WHAT to do ABOUT Holly

Also by Joan Lingard and published by Catnip:
The Eleventh Orphan
The File on Fraulein Berg

WHAT to do ABOUT Holly

JOAN LINGARD

Catnip

For Lindsey Fraser

CATNIP BOOKS
Published by Catnip Publishing Ltd
14 Greville Street
London EC1N 8SB

This edition first published 2009
1 3 5 7 9 10 8 6 4 2

Text copyright © Joan Lingard, 2009

The moral right of the author has been asserted

A CIP catalogue record for this book is available from the British Library

ISBN 978-1-84647-090-5

Printed in Poland

www.catnippublishing.co.uk

One

'Come on, Holly,' said her mother, grabbing her free hand. 'And stop dragging yer feet or you'll miss yer train.'

'I'm not wantin' to go on the train on my own.'

'Well, you'll just have to, won't you? I can't take you. I've my work to go to.'

Queen Street Station was heaving with people. It was late afternoon on a Friday. Half of Glasgow seemed to be there, on the move, coming and going, milling about, heading for the trains. A man jiggled Holly's elbow and slopped his carton of coffee. He gave her a glare as if it were her fault. She glared back to let him know he couldn't get away with it.

Sharon, Holly's mum, kept a firm hold of her hand, tugging her on in the direction of the platforms.

'What would you do, Sylvie? If you were me?' asked Holly.

Sylvie wasn't too keen to go either. The train would be packed. Holly's mother couldn't just throw her on board, could she, like a parcel? Especially in front of all those people. She'd get arrested.

'Mum,' said Holly, coming to a dead halt, 'I'm not goin' unless you come with me.'

Sharon turned to face her daughter. 'You're just being silly. And was that you talking to yer so-called friend again?'

'She's not *so*-called. Her name's Sylvie.'

'It's not right, talking to somebody who's not there.'

Holly didn't answer. As far as she was concerned, Sylvie *was* there, all the time, inside her head, whenever she needed someone to talk to.

Sharon sighed and took a deep breath.

'You want to see your dad, don't you?'

Holly shrugged. She could see her mother might snap any minute.

'You know you do,' Sylvie reminded her. 'You can't wait to see him. You said so.'

'I don't know what I'm goin' to do wi' you, Holly,' her mother went on.

'It's the goin' on the train on my own, Mum. Why don't you come with me?'

'It'd cost me a full return fare, for a start, and I'm skint. Besides, you know I can't afford to lose my job. I have to feed and clothe you!'

'Dad pays you.'

That only annoyed Sharon more. 'Not for everything he doesn't.'

'I could pay for your ticket. I've saved up my pocket money.'

'She doesn't start work till nine, does she?' put in Sylvie. 'And it's not five yet.'

'You'd have plenty of time,' said Holly.

'I've told you, it'd cost me, and I'm not letting you pay.' Sharon then changed her voice and Holly knew she was going to try coaxing. 'Listen, luv, you've been on the train before. I'll find a nice older lady for you to sit

2

beside, the way I did last time. Somebody to keep an eye on you.'

'I didn't like it but.'

'No harm can come to you on a train full of folk. It's only for forty-five minutes. And your dad'll be waitin' at the other end to pick you up.'

Holly still didn't move.

'Boy, are you stubborn!' Sharon shook her head. 'Just like your dad! And as for that stupid Sylvie, it's time you got rid of her!'

'She is *not* stupid! She's the cleverest girl in her class. *And* she can play the viola.'

Sharon ignored that. She tried her wheedling voice again. 'You'll have a great time with your dad. He spoils you rotten, you know he does.'

'I haven't seen him for yonks. I might not recognize him,' said Holly.

'Don't talk rubbish!'

'*That* was rubbish,' murmured Sylvie.

'For crying out loud – !' Sharon was about to lose her rag. 'You're not a baby any longer. You're eleven years old!'

'Just,' put in Sylvie.

Holly'd had her birthday only the week before.

Her mother carried on. 'I went on the train to Greenock to visit my Auntie Nessie when I was half your age.'

'You were a child wonder, so you were,' said Holly. She'd read that phrase in a book. She picked up a lot of things from books.

'Don't you be cheeky to me, madam!'

'But it was probably illegal, your mum putting you on

the train when you were six,' Holly pointed out, though she knew her mum hadn't meant it, not exactly.

'You've always got a smart answer, haven't you?'

'You're riling her,' said Sylvie.

'I don't know what's got into you lately!' exploded Sharon. 'Don't tell me you're turning into a teenager before your time!'

They were attracting more and more annoyed looks. People kept bumping into them. They were in the way.

'Come on!' snapped Sharon, then she yanked Holly forward without looking back. Holly was forced to pick up her bag and her feet and move. Her mum was not going to give in.

'And she says you and your dad are the stubborn ones!' tutted Sylvie.

They found their platform. Passengers stood three, four, five deep, waiting for the Edinburgh train. Sharon trawled along, towing Holly behind her, eyeing all the faces, looking for a nice lady. People gave way to let them through but they didn't look overly pleased about it. Holly kept her head down.

Sharon stopped halfway along the platform, glancing about her. She hadn't seen a suitable lady yet. She'd know there would be no point in asking any of the youngish business women in black suits carrying briefcases. They didn't want to be saddled with a child. Sharon pursed her lips and eyed her watch.

Then Holly looked up and saw someone she recognized standing by herself further up the platform. The woman recognized her and smiled and Holly waved back shyly.

'Who's that you're wavin' to?' Sharon frowned as if she were trying to remember something.

'Her name's Nina Nightingale.'

'Nina Nightingale? Funny sort of name.'

'What's funny about it?' Holly thought it was a lovely name. So did Sylvie. Well, Sylvie would, wouldn't she?

'How do you know her?' Sharon turned to inspect the woman.

'Don't stare at her, Mum! It's rude.'

'I'm not starin'. I'm just lookin'. When did you meet her?'

'She was at our school today.'

'I thought I'd seen her before! She came out the gate when I was waiting for you. What was she doin' there?'

'She came to talk to our class. She's a writer.'

'A *writer*?'

'My *favourite* writer. I brought a letter home from school saying she was comin'. I asked you to give me some money to buy a book but you wouldn't.' They'd had a row about that.

'I'd nothin' to spare, I told you. You've lots of books, anyway.'

Holly had bought one anyway, without letting on to her mother. She'd had three pounds fifty of her own saved up and she took the rest out of her mother's purse when she wasn't looking. She'd decided it was different from stealing to buy things that were bad for you, like sweets. Anyway, her mother'd had plenty of money in her purse. It was just that she thought there was no point in buying a book when you could get it out of the library

5

for nothing. But Holly had desperately wanted one of Nina Nightingale's books to keep. And so had Sylvie. Sylvie would have been mad if she hadn't bought it, especially as it was one of the stories where she was the main character.

'So you know her then?' Sharon was looking thoughtful.

'Well, sort of.'

'She must be goin' to Edinburgh. Looks like she's on her own too. Did she say where she lived?'

'I think it was Edinburgh.' Holly was beginning to feel alarmed. Surely her mother wasn't going to dump her on a famous writer!

'She looks quite nice,' commented Sharon. 'I'm sure she wouldn't mind keeping an eye on you. It is only for forty-five minutes after all.'

'Mu-um,' wailed Holly, but her mother was already on the move again, saying, 'Excuse me, excuse me!' and pushing her way through the crowds as she headed in a straight line for Nina Nightingale.

When they were closing in on the writer Sharon paused to hiss in her daughter's ear, 'Now behave yoursel' when you're with her! Dinna be letting me down! See and speak proper! You can do it when you want. And keep hold of your ticket! I can't afford another.'

'There's no stopping your mum when she gets going,' observed Sylvie. 'She's like a tornado.'

Holly's stomach was churning.

'Excuse me,' Sharon said again and on reaching the writer tapped her on the arm to get her attention.

Nina Nightingale turned. She looked surprised but she gave Holly another smile.

'Hello there! You were at my talk. You bought one of my books, didn't you? And I signed it for you. I seem to remember your name's Holly? Am I right?'

Holly nodded. Her face felt as if it were on fire.

'Holly just loves books to bits,' said Sharon, putting on an accent that she thought was 'posh', which made Holly feel even worse. 'She's always got her head stuck in one. Sometimes I says to her to away out and play and she says she wants to get on with her book!'

'Books are good things to love,' said Nina Nightingale. 'At least, I think so! But I would, wouldn't I?'

She laughed and then so did Sharon. Sharon laughed too much, too loudly, as if it was the best joke she'd heard in years. Holly didn't laugh. She was trying to work out how to escape. It would be difficult to do a runner here with so many people in the way.

'Anyway,' Nina Nightingale went on, 'it was very kind of you to give Holly the money to buy one of my books. I appreciate that.'

'I always say you can't spend your money on nothing better,' said Sharon, avoiding her daughter's eye.

The passengers were leaning to the left, gazing along the platform. The Edinburgh train had been sighted in the distance.

'Miss Nightingale,' said Sharon hurriedly, 'would you happen to be going to Edinburgh?'

The writer didn't seem to know what she should say.

'Mu-um,' wailed Holly.

'Well, yes, I am.' Nina Nightingale looked slightly puzzled.

They could hear the rumble of the train now.

'I've got a problem, you see, Miss Nightingale,' gabbled Sharon. 'I wonder if you could help me out? I'm in a bit of a fix.'

'Mu-um,' pleaded Holly but her mother ignored her and carried on talking as the noise of the train grew steadily louder.

'Holly's dad's picking her up at the other end in Edinburgh but I can't go with her on the train 'cos I've got my work to go to. Usually I wouldn't let her go on her own but this is an emergency.'

The engine chugged past them and then came the first of the carriages. The train began to slow and passengers started to surge forward. Holly and her mother and the writer had to step back to get out of their way.

'If you could just keep an eye on her,' continued Sharon, her voice almost drowned out by the announcement overhead and the clamour going on all around them. 'I'd be awfy, grateful so I would.'

'Well, I suppose,' began Nina but got no further.

'Thanks a million, Miss Nightingale,' said Sharon. 'You're a star.' She turned and gave Holly a quick hug and a kiss. 'Now you be a good girl and I'll see you soon. OK, darlin'?'

With that, Sharon fled back along the platform on her spiky four-inch heels, her blond ponytail bouncing up and down. Holly wanted to run after her but didn't.

It was as if her feet were stuck to the platform.

'Well, Holly,' said Nina Nightingale, 'we'd better get on board, hadn't we?'

'I suppose we'd better,' said Holly silently to Sylvie.

'We've no choice, have we?' returned Sylvie.

They were the last passengers to board the 5 o'clock train to Edinburgh.

Two

They had to walk almost the entire length of the train before they found two seats together. The writer let Holly sit by the window while she took the aisle seat.

Holly sat close in to the window, clutching her star-spangled pink bag. She could see herself in the glass. Her face looked pale, like a ghost's. Her fair hair was held back in a pink scrunch to make a ponytail, the same as her mum's. It kept flopping on to her shoulder and she had to keep flicking it back. She felt like a parcel that had been dumped on someone who didn't want her. Nina hadn't had any chance to say no, had she?

'She's a kind woman,' said Sylvie. 'She won't be minding.'

'Are you all right there, Holly?' asked Nina. 'With your bag on your lap?'

'You see,' said Sylvie, 'she wants you to be comfy.'

'Uh-huh,' said Holly, and then, after a moment's thought, added, 'Yes, thank you,' in a proper sort of voice.

The train had pulled out of the station and was gradually picking up speed. Soon they were rolling through the outskirts of Glasgow past high-rise flats.

'Do you go to Edinburgh often?' asked Nina.

Holly shook her head.

'But your dad lives there?'

'He's got a flat.' It wouldn't be quite true to say that he lived there.

'Is that his home?'

'Sort of. He's not there much.'

'I see,' said Nina though she obviously didn't. 'Where is he most of the time?'

'He works in the oil.'

'Ah. Up in Aberdeen?'

'No, abroad. Somewhere.' Holly added limply.

'The Middle East?'

'Think so.' She really didn't know.

'But he's back in Edinburgh at present? On leave?'

Holly nodded. Perhaps Nina would stop asking her questions now.

'Sorry.' Nina smiled at Holly. 'We writers like to know about other people's lives. My son Johnny complains when I quiz his friends!'

The attendant with the drinks trolley came round. 'Anyone for teas, coffee, soft drinks?'

'Fancy something to drink, Holly?' asked Nina.

Holly lifted one shoulder in a shrug.

'I'm going to have a cup of coffee,' said Nina. 'What about some orange juice?'

She ordered a coffee for herself and an orange juice and a wrapped chocolate biscuit for Holly.

'Thank you,' said Holly politely. She held out the biscuit. 'You could have half if you want?'

'I'm not hungry, thanks.'

Holly ate the biscuit and drank the juice. She was glad of both. She was hungry. She hadn't eaten much lunch. She'd been worrying about getting on the train to Edinburgh.

'Told you Nina was kind, didn't I?' said Sylvie.

The train travelled on. It was warm in the compartment. The two women facing them across the table had dropped off to sleep. One of them was snoring. Several people were talking on mobile phones.

And then Nina's rang. She fished around in her handbag until she found it. The inside of her bag didn't look any tidier than Sharon's.

'Hi, Colin,' said Nina, pressing the phone to one ear and covering the other with her hand. It was so noisy in the carriage that she must be having a problem hearing. 'I'm on the five o'clock. No, don't bother to meet me. I'll take a taxi.' She listened for a moment before continuing, 'Go out for a meal? Sounds like a good idea. Save cooking. Johnny's going to Tim's tonight anyway. They're having a barbecue and he's sleeping over so we're free. See you soon. Bye.' She clicked off the phone and put it back in her bag.

'That was my husband,' she said to Holly.

Holly had gathered that.

'You must be pleased it's the holidays?' said Nina.

Holly nodded.

'Are you spending both weeks with your dad?' The questions had started again.

'Not sure. Depends.'

'All tickets please!' The ticket inspector had entered the carriage. Nina took her ticket out of her wallet. Holly began to rummage in her coat pocket. She was sure she'd put it there.

'What's wrong?' asked Nina. 'Can't you find your ticket?'

'I put it in my pocket.' Holly dug into the other one. Her face was flushed.

'You're sure you didn't put it in your bag?'

'Don't think so.'

'Maybe you'd better look?'

Holly unzipped the bag and poked around amongst a jumble of clothes and books. Then she tried her all pockets again.

'I must've lost it,' she cried forlornly. 'My mum'll kill me!'

'Let's look under the table. You might have dropped it.'

They scrabbled around on the floor trying not to bang their heads on the table. The only thing they found was the wrapper from Holly's chocolate biscuit.

The two of them surfaced, hot in the face, to find that the inspector had reached their row. He was waiting with his hand held out. And he didn't look patient. He had a lot of passengers to check. Nina handed over her ticket.

'I've lost mine!' Holly looked up into the man's face. 'But my mum bought me one, honest she did, in the station.'

'You can't travel without a ticket,' said the inspector. He turned to Nina. 'I'm afraid you'll have to buy another, madam. At full fare.'

Nina opened her wallet again.

'You can't pay for me, Nina,' cried Holly.

Nina had told them they could call her by her Christian name before she'd started her talk to them at school. 'I've got some money of my own.'

She produced a pink purse from her bag and coins spilled out of it on to the table top. Nina caught one before it bounced over the edge.

'It's all right, Holly. I'll pay for your ticket just now and your dad can pay me back when we get to Edinburgh.'

Holly protested again but Nina handed the money over to the inspector.

'Thanks.' muttered Holly, her face heating up again. She wouldn't look like a ghost now.

'It's not a problem, dear.'

Holly tried to sit as still as she could. She didn't want to make any more trouble.

The train stopped at Falkirk, Linlithgow, and then at Haymarket. Passengers got on and off.

'Next stop Waverley,' came the announcement on the tannoy overhead and the remaining passengers began to get up and pull down their coats and bags from the luggage racks. The two women across the table came back to life with a jerk.

'Nearly there,' said Nina brightly. She looked tired. She must be looking forward to going out for a nice meal with her husband, thought Holly.

The train emerged from a long tunnel and, running at a slower rate now, cut through Princes Street gardens. Squinting out of the window Edinburgh Castle could be seen standing high above them on its rock.

'It looks like a nice evening,' said Nina.

The sun was shining.

'We are now approaching Waverley Station,' said the voice on the tannoy. 'Please make sure you have all your possessions with you. Thank you for travelling with First ScotRail today.'

Holly held her bag ever more tightly to her chest, worried that she might lose something else. She felt edgy and a bit nervous. It was ages since she'd seen her dad.

'Relax,' said Sylvie. 'You know it'll be fine once you see him.'

And it always was. He'd open his arms to her and she'd run into them and he'd hold her tight and laugh and say, 'You're getting to be a big girl, Holly!'

She wasn't really that big. In fact, Holly was the smallest in her class. Some of the girls who were like lampposts called her Titch. Her mum said to pay no notice to them but it was all right for her to talk! She wore four-inch heels to make herself look taller. She said Holly could do the same when she was older.

Nina waited until the train had come to a halt before she stood up. She lifted down her briefcase, stood out into the aisle and waited for Holly to join her.

'Will your dad be on the platform or at the barrier?'

'At the barrier. He says that way he won't miss me.'

They let those who were in a hurry go past.

'No point in getting killed in the rush,' said Nina.

Holly bit her fingernails. They tasted of her mother's pink nail polish. It was a bit sickly.

'Stop that!' ordered Sylvie.

Holly dropped her hand.

'I think we can go now.' Nina led the way out of the carriage. They were amongst the last to get off but the platform was swarming with passengers waiting to board the train, which would then shuttle back to Glasgow.

They followed the stream of people moving steadily in the direction of the barriers and went through them into the station. The concourse was just as hectic as the one in Glasgow had been.

'Friday afternoon is certainly not a good time to travel,' remarked Nina.

Holly stood on tiptoe, scanning the crowds.

'See any sign of your dad?'

Holly shook her head.

'Not to worry. He could have got caught up in all the traffic.'

A whistle blew somewhere behind them and the train for Glasgow moved off.

After another few minutes Nina asked Holly if her dad would have known which train she'd be on.

'My mum sent him an email. She told him I'd be on the 5 o'clock from Glasgow.'

Holly saw Nina take a quick look at the station clock. Their train had come in bang on time at a quarter to six. It was now almost five past.

'Plenty of time yet, ' said Nina, sounding a little ruffled.

They continued to wait. Holly's eyes continued to rove around the station.

'Anyone can be late,' said Sylvie, trying to be reassuring.

By the time the hands of the station clock stood at twenty past, Nina was looking distinctly uneasy.

'Would he come by car? Your dad?'

'Dunno. Sometimes he rents one when he comes back. Sometimes he just jumps on the bus. Says it saves parking.' Holly felt her voice croaking at the back of her throat.

'Very sensible.'

At half-past six Nina said, 'I think perhaps we should phone him. Do you have his number?'

Holly had it written on a piece of paper in her pocket. It was a landline number, probably the phone in the flat. Nina dialled it on her mobile and waited. She pursed her lips.

'No answer. That might be because he's on his way of course. Has he ever been late before?'

'Not really.'

'That's not a proper answer,' reproved Sylvie.

'No, he hasn't,' added Holly.

Nina frowned. 'You don't think your mum might have got the time of the train wrong?'

'She said five. I watched her write the email. I usually help her with the spelling.'

'In that case I think we'd better phone her.'

'She's lost her mobile. It got nicked at her work. She was going to get a new one today after she'd seen me on to the train.'

'So you won't know that number ..? Do you have a landline phone at home?'

Holly shook her head.

'Where does your mum work?'

'The *Spike*.'

'The *Spike*?'

'It's a club. But she doesn't go there till just before nine o'clock.'

'I see.' Nina was considering her next move. 'I'd better phone my husband.'

She moved a few steps away from Holly and turned her back while she made the call. Holly leaned in to hear. She was good at eavesdropping. Her mum said she was too nosey for her own good. Sylvie said maybe Holly would be a writer when she grew up.

'I'm going to be a little late, Colin,' Nina was saying. There was quite a din in the station. She raised her voice and repeated, shouting almost, 'I'm going to be late. Yes, *late*! I've got a bit of a problem and I don't know what to do about it…'

She half turned to look back. Holly wished she could drop through a hole in the ground.

Three

'What are we going to do, Sylvie?' asked Holly.

Sylvie had no suggestions at the moment. She'd have to think about it. Usually she had plenty of ideas for getting out of tight corners. She'd had to do it often enough herself in Nina's stories. When she'd been on the trail of egg thieves she'd almost been cornered by one of them and had had to run for her life.

Nina was still talking on her mobile to her husband. She was pacing up and down at the same time, keeping well away from them, so that they wouldn't be able to hear what she was saying.

When she'd finished talking, she came back and said, 'My husband's coming down to collect us. If your dad hasn't made an appearance by then, Holly, we'll run you down to his house. He might have got the date wrong!'

'My mum said Friday on the email.'

'But sometimes people can write the wrong day down in their diary. I've done it myself.'

'I don't know if he has a diary.' Holly supposed he might, out there on his oil rig. She couldn't imagine what that would be like.

'There must be some reason that he's not here. You said he's never done this before?'

'Never.' Holly shook her head. 'No, honest, not ever.'
She didn't want Nina thinking her dad was useless.

'Well, let's go and see if we can leave a message for him
at the station manager's office. In case he turns up after
we've gone.'

Nina set off with Holly and Sylvie trailing behind.

'Of course you can leave a message,' said the woman
in the office. She held a pen poised over a pad of paper,
waiting for instructions.

'What's your dad's name, Holly?' asked Nina.

'Joe. Joe Hamilton.'

The woman wrote that down.

'So,' said Nina, 'could you tell him, please, if he turns
up looking for his daughter Holly that he should phone
me, Nina Nightingale, at this number?'

If he turns up! Holly gulped.

'He always has before, hasn't he?' said Sylvie.

The woman wrote the names and number down, then
read them back so that Nina could double check. 'I'll see
he gets it,' she said.

'Thank you very much. I'd be most grateful.'

Where was he? Maybe something had happened to
him, Holly thought. He could have had an accident,
fallen off the oil rig. He might be lying in a hospital
right this very minute. Or else, if he'd got as far as
Edinburgh, he could have been hit by a lorry when
he was getting off the bus. He could be dead. Holly's
mind went on churning. Sylvie said she was letting

her imagination run away with her, something she often did herself.

Back in the main part of the station they halted in front of the big clock. The hands now showed it to be five minutes past seven, and they were always right, weren't they? Holly stared up at them, watching the big hand slide over to six, then seven, then eight minutes past. Even if her dad had thought she was coming on the 6 o'clock train he should have been here by now. He must have had an accident and died. All of a sudden it was too much for her. Holly burst into tears.

'Something's happened to him. I know he wouldn't just leave me here.'

Nina put an arm round her shoulder and said, 'It's OK, love, don't worry about it. I'm sure it's just a mix-up. These things happen sometimes.'

'I'm sorry,' sobbed Holly.

'It's not your fault.'

Holly sniffed and took the tissue Nina was holding out. She was furious with herself for crying like that in front of a famous writer. She'd think she was a right cry-baby!

'Don't worry,' said Sylvie. 'It'll give her something to write about in her next book.'

At twenty minutes past seven a red car came down the ramp into the station and pulled up.

'That's Colin, my husband,' cried Nina, sounding relieved. 'Come on then, Holly! Have you got your bag there?'

A man got out of the car and Nina introduced the two of them.

'Holly, this is my husband, Colin.' He was a big, broad-shouldered man.

'Pleased to meet you, Holly,' he said.

Like heck he is, thought Holly. He probably wished she'd vanish in a puff of smoke. She wished she could too. And she had another problem, a more pressing one. She jiggled from foot to foot.

'Are you OK, Holly?' asked Nina, frowning.

'I need to go to the toilet,' mumbled Holly, keeping her head down. Her mum had told her to go in the station in Glasgow but she hadn't needed then.

'That's all right. Colin will wait, won't you, dear?'

'I'll just move the car. I'm a bit in the way here.'

A taxi was honking behind them.

'We're causing nothing but trouble,' Holly said to Sylvie. 'Mum would have a fit if she saw me.'

Nina conducted Holly to the toilets, paid for them both to go in and promised to wait for her by the washhand basins.

'I'll hold your bag for you,' she offered.

Holly surrendered it unwillingly. She didn't like letting go of it but she didn't like to refuse.

Inside the cubicle, Sylvie was furious. 'This is a fine mess we've got ourselves in!' But she knew Holly was worried, 'I expect your dad will turn up, though, at some point.'

'He'd better!'

When Holly had finished she went straightaway to a basin and washed her hands thoroughly, taking her time. She was sure Nina would approve of that. Her own mum was very fussy about hand-washing. She'd said you could get a nasty bug called E-coli if you didn't do it properly.

Holly looked at herself in the mirror and then wished she hadn't. She had a smudge on her nose and some of her hair had come loose from its ponytail. What a sight! Perhaps she'd better wash her face too…

'Don't take too long, Holly,' urged Nina. 'You look clean enough. Colin will be waiting.'

Holly dried her hands on the back of her trousers and followed Nina out. They found her husband in a parking space round the back of the platforms.

'Hop in, then,' he said, opening the back door of the car for Holly. She slid in with her bag, and Sylvie. It wasn't often they got the chance of a ride in a car so they might as well sit back and enjoy themselves. Nina got into the front. She turned round.

'You do know where your dad lives, don't you, Holly?'

Course she did! 'Down the bottom of Leith Walk.'

'You know the number?'

'206.'

'Leith Walk's not far anyway,' said Colin cheerfully. 'We'll be there in no time.'

He seemed quite a jolly man. Sylvie said it was just as well! Holly relaxed a little.

When they'd got their seat belts on, Colin drove back up the ramp and into the streets of Edinburgh. They turned along Princes Street and down into Leith Walk. It was a long, wide street.

'Right down at the bottom, did you say, Holly?' asked Colin.

'Almost.' She'd only visited her father there twice. He'd just bought the flat a few months ago.

Colin parked once he found a space near the foot of the street. They got out and began to walk. Nina read the numbers aloud. '164, 166… Even numbers, so it must be this side.' They continued on down.

'I don't think it's this far.' Holly squinted back up the street.

'We'd better carry on down though,' said Nina.

At 198 they stopped. It was the last number in the street.

'Are you *sure* it's 206?' asked Nina.

'I'm sure that's what my mum told me,' Holly replied.

'Looks like she may have got it wrong, then.' Colin was still sounding cheery but his wife was looking tired. Maybe even fed up, thought Sylvie. You couldn't blame her.

'It's got a blue door,' said Holly desperately. She was beginning to feel really quite panic-stricken.

'I don't suppose there will be all that many blue doors at the bottom of Leith Walk!' said Colin. 'Let's have a recce, shall we?'

They retraced their steps.

'That's it!' cried Holly, spotting a familiar door. It *was* blue!

She ran towards it, followed by Colin and Nina. There was a row of buzzers at the side of the door, most of which had names on them.

'Is your dad's name there?' asked Nina.

'Hamilton!' announced Holly triumphantly, pointing to it at the top of the list of names. There it was, proof that he lived there and she'd not been fibbing!

'Bravo!' declared Colin.

'Thank goodness,' murmured Nina.

'My mum must have got the number wrong. She's a bit scattery-brained at times.' Holly laughed. It was the first time she'd felt like laughing since she'd left Glasgow.

'Perhaps your dad possibly never got her email. That would explain why he wasn't at the station.'

'Let's hope he's in then!' said Colin.

Holly hoped so too. As did Sylvie, of course. Holly pressed the bell and got ready to speak into the intercom.

They waited. Nothing happened.

'Try again,' urged Colin.

Holly pressed the bell hard and held it down for a few seconds.

'Watch you don't break it,' cautioned Colin, with a smile.

Nina was being very quiet.

After the third try Colin said, 'I don't think he can be in.'

'I'm afraid neither do I.' said Nina.

'He might have nipped out to the shops,' suggested Holly.

On the other hand, as Sylvie countered, he might not.

'What about trying one of the neighbours?' Colin was studying the names beside the buzzers. 'Somebody might know where he is.'

'There's a Mrs McGinty, top right, just across the

landing from my dad,' said Holly. 'He's top left. My dad said she knows everything that happens on the stair. She takes in parcels and things like that for him when he's not there.'

Holly's dad had told her that Mrs McGinty was a right nosey parker but she was helpful to have around. Holly didn't think Colin and Nina needed to know any of that.

'Mrs McGinty's our woman then,' declared Colin and reached out to ring the bell himself. They didn't have to wait long.

'Who's there?' demanded a voice issuing from the intercom.

'That's her!' cried Holly.

'We're looking for a Mr Joe Hamilton,' said Colin.

'Oh, aye. What are ye wantin' wi' him?'

'We have his daughter Holly here. Do you think we could come up and have a word with you?'

'Push the door!'

They entered the dimly lit stairway and climbed the three flights of stairs, with Holly leading the way. As they reached the third flight they saw a small elderly woman standing in a lit doorway.

'You must be Mrs McGinty,' said Colin, extending his hand to her. 'My name's Colin Nightingale and this is my wife Nina. And this, as you will know, is Holly.'

Mrs McGinty looked taken aback at being offered a hand to shake but she took it anyway.

She addressed Holly, 'So you're looking for your dad, are you?'

'I've come to stay with him for my holidays.'

'Well, you'll just need to gang back hame again. He's no here.' The woman sounded triumphant.

'Not here?' repeated Nina.

'Do you mean he's out for the evening?' asked Colin.

'No, he's away on some oil rig somewhere, raking in the dough.'

'But we understood that he would be home on leave?' said Nina.

'He was supposed to be coming the now but something come up on the rig so he had to change his plans. He sent me a postcard.'

Sent *you* a postcard? thought Holly.

'When is he coming back then?' asked Colin. 'Do you know?'

'Aye. Two weeks tomorrow.'

'Two weeks,' echoed Nina.

Holly gulped. There was an uncomfortable silence during which Sylvie proposed that they cut and run. Running off had always worked out for her. That would let Nina off the hook.

'But where could we run to?' Holly asked her friend.

Four

There was really no chance at all of doing a runner. Holly had the feeling that if she tried Colin would be after her in a flash. His wife was looking fraught. She must have had to catch an early train to Glasgow, thought Holly. She'd given a talk to Holly's class that morning, and another one in the afternoon.

'It's no wonder she's tired,' sighed Sylvie. 'And now she's got you on her hands and doesn't know what to do about you.'

'What time did you say your mum started work, Holly?' asked Nina.

'Nine.'

'Let's go home then. We can phone her from our house.'

Mrs McGinty sniffed. 'Her! She's a right flighty one that, from what I've heard.'

Holly saw Nina giving the woman an annoyed look. Holly gave her one too. Nasty old bat that she was! She'd no right speaking about her mum like that in front of strangers! In front of anybody. Her dad would soon tick her off if he were there. If only!

Where was he? Had he changed his mind? Maybe he wasn't on a rig, but had decided to go somewhere nice for his holidays. Maybe he didn't want to see her any more.

'Don't be silly,' chided Sylvie. 'Remember he wrote

you a postcard after your last visit saying how much he'd enjoyed his holiday with you?'

Holly had pinned the postcard to her wall.

'Perhaps we should leave a note for your dad, Holly,' suggested Colin. 'Got a piece of paper, Nina? I'm sure you must have.'

Nina had a notebook in her bag. She always carried one, in case an idea came to her unexpectedly. She'd told them so in her talk that morning. It was a tip for anyone wanting to write. Funnily enough, Holly had always kept a notebook herself. She liked to watch people from her window and imagine what they were doing or where they were going. Her mum said if any crime happened in the street Holly would be able to help the police! So far nothing much had happened, apart from people dropping litter, or letting their dogs soil the pavement. But she kept hoping for something really exciting.

Mrs McGinty edged closer to watch as Nina tore out a page and wrote a quick note.

'I've given your dad our phone number,' she told Holly, 'and explained what happened and who we are.'

'I can give it to him for you.' Mrs McGinty held out her hand ready to take the note.

'It's fine, thanks.' Nina was polite, though there was an edge to her voice. 'We wouldn't want to trouble you any more than we have. I'll just put it through the letter box.'

'Whatever you want.' Mrs McGinty folded her arms across her chest. She was not pleased. She was a woman who was seldom pleased about anything, unless it was picking up gossip or slagging somebody off. There were one or two like her in Holly's street in Glasgow too.

Nina popped the note through the letter box.

'Thanks for your help, Mrs McGinty,' said Colin and led the way back down the stairs.

'Mind you close the bottom door properly behind you,' Mrs McGinty called after them. 'I'm no wanting any drunks getting into the stair and messin' it up.'

'Makes you feel you'd like to leave it wide open,' muttered Nina.

Holly gave her a grin.

They did, however, shut the door.

'She'll be watching us from her window.' Holly peered up. 'To see what kind of car you've got.'

'Let her watch all she wants!' declared Colin. 'A fat lot of good it'll do her.'

It had started to rain. They dived for the car.

'I don't know about the two of you but I'm ravenous,' announced Nina, once they were inside.

'Why don't we buy some pizza on the way home,' said Colin. 'Do you like pizza, Holly?'

'Yes, thank you.'

But she was feeling uncomfortable again. She didn't want them to have to buy her pizza. It didn't seem right.

'You've just got to go along with it,' said Sylvie. 'What else can you do?'

They stopped at a pizza place and Colin invited Holly to come in with him so that she could choose the toppings she wanted. Nina said she'd like bacon, peppers and mushroom on hers.

Holly picked cheese and pepperoni. 'I always have that,' she said, quietly. 'My best friend does too.' She and Sylvie liked the same things.

They had to wait for a few minutes while their order was being prepared. Colin chatted to the man at the counter and when the pizzas were ready he passed the money over.

'My dad'll pay you back,' said Holly.

'No need. This is our treat.'

'Are you sure?'

'Of course! Would you mind having the pizzas on the back seat with you?'

Holly didn't mind at all. She kept her hand on the warm boxes so that they didn't slide off the seat. The smell made her mouth water as they drove across town.

The Nightingales lived in a large Victorian house on the south side of the city, not far from the green open space known as the Meadows. Holly thought she might have been to a fair there once with her dad.

Nina was obviously relieved to be home. She threw her jacket over the back of a chair and kicked off her shoes, giving a sigh of relief. They sat at the big wooden kitchen table and she and Colin had a glass of wine with their pizzas while Holly was offered apple juice. They were all starving. No one spoke until they'd finished eating.

'That feels better,' declared Nina, sitting back.

'What about another glass of wine?' offered Colin.

Nina held out her glass. 'I feel I've earned it.'

'You gave a lovely talk,' said Holly shyly. 'Everybody else thought so too.'

'Thank you, dear.' Nina smiled. 'I'm glad you did.'

When she'd finished her wine she said, 'I think it's time to ring your mother, Holly.'

'She'll be hoppin' mad. Not with you,' Holly added quickly. 'With my dad. She'll go her dinger.'

'We don't yet know whose fault it is, though, do we? Do you have the number of that club?'

She should have it somewhere but it seemed to have gone the same way as the train ticket. At least, she couldn't find it in the pink bag or any of her coat or jean pockets. She turned them all inside out.

'I must have pulled it out my pocket in the station.' Holly felt flustered.

'Not to worry,' said Colin. 'We can get it from Directory Enquiries.'

'I'm giving you an awful lot of bother.'

'It won't take a minute.' Colin said and smiled reassuringly.

The Nightingales had a phone mounted on the wall in the kitchen. Colin lifted the receiver and dialled. His call was answered quickly.

'A miracle,' he said, covering the receiver briefly with his hand. 'What town? Glasgow. Name? The *Spike*. Yes – S – P – I – K – E.' He covered the receiver again. 'Address, Holly?'

'Buchanan Street. No, Sauchiehall Street. I think,' she added. 'Somewhere in the middle of the town?'

'Sauchiehall Street,' Colin repeated. He waited. Then he frowned. 'Can you try Buchanan Street?' Another pause. 'You can't find the name at all? It's a club. It must be listed. Can you try again please, in case I've got the address wrong? It's urgent.'

Nina and Holly sat without saying a word, watching him. Holly bit her nails. Not that there was much for her to get her teeth into.

'Stop it!' cried Sylvie.

'You're absolutely certain it's not there?' Colin was frowning. 'Well, thanks for trying.' He replaced the receiver and turned to look at them.

'But my mum works there,' cried Holly. 'I know she does, I've been there.'

'Are you sure it's called the *Spike*?' asked Nina.

Holly paused and then she felt her face flaming up again.

'You're not, are you?' said Nina gently.

'Its real name is the *Silver Spike* but mum always just says the *Spike*. I'm sorry, I never thought.' Holly felt herself getting hot.

'That explains it, at any rate,' said Colin. 'I can understand why you wouldn't have remembered. I'll have another go at it.'

He dialled again and this time had to wait for a couple of minutes before someone came on the line. He asked for the right place this time and held his thumb up to let Nina and Holly know he was being successful. He repeated the numbers aloud and Nina wrote them down.

'Thank you very much,' he said and hung up.

'I think I'd better speak to Holly's mum.' Nina got up and Colin handed her the phone.

Colin read the Glasgow numbers out while she dialled.

'It's ringing!' she announced. She waited. It was obviously going on ringing.

'Sometimes they take ages to answer,' put in Holly. 'It being a club. They don't hear the phone, you see. The music's so loud.'

'Can imagine,' murmured Colin.

'Do you have to ring your mum there sometimes?' asked Nina, who was still listening with the receiver at her ear.

'Sometimes,' muttered Holly.

She knew what they'd be thinking: that she was left alone in the house while her mother went to work. Well, maybe it was true, but her mum had to work and Norma across the landing was always at home if she needed anything.

Nina leant back against the wall, the phone still against her ear.

'She really is exhausted,' commented Sylvie.

Holly could see that.

Nina came to with a jolt when someone finally answered at the other end. 'Is that the *Silver Spike*? It is?' She turned to Holly. 'What's your mum's name, dear?'

'Sharon.'

'Could I speak to Sharon Hamilton please?' asked Nina.

'It's not Hamilton,' put in Holly quickly. 'I should have said. She's called Anderson.'

'Sorry,' said Nina, raising her voice a notch, 'Sharon Anderson.' She listened, then said, as if she couldn't believe it, 'Sharon's not in tonight? *Not at all*? Are you sure?'

Holly got up and went to stand near Nina. She was trembling as she did so.

'Do you know where I might contact her? It's about her daughter Holly. *Holly*,' Nina repeated. 'Her daughter.' She covered the mouthpiece with her hand and said, 'You were right about the music! You can hardly make out what they're saying.'

'My mum's not there, is she?' Holly's voice wobbled.

'It's probably a mistake, love. Don't worry about it. He's gone to get someone called Chrissie.'

'She and my mum are pals.'

It was taking a while for Chrissie to come to the phone.

'Maybe she's not there either tonight,' said Nina. A few moments passed. 'Oh no, here she is!' She spoke into the receiver again. 'My name is Nina Nightingale,' she went on to explain how Holly had come to be in her care. 'So you'll understand that I'm anxious to contact her mother, Sharon. I'm trying to find out where she might be right now?'

Silence while Chrissie spoke.

'Gone on –' Nina began and then stopped. She glanced over at Colin. 'For how long?'

'Where's she gone?' cried Holly.

'*Couple of* –' Nina stopped again. 'Can you tell me where? You don't know? Right. You wouldn't have a mobile number for her? You don't? Yes, Holly said she was having to buy a new one. Have you any idea how I might get hold of Holly's father?'

'She doesn't know him,' interrupted Holly. 'She's never met him.'

'Are you sure she's gone away?' asked Nina.

Chrissie was talking now.

'That would be helpful,' said Nina. 'I'll give you our number. Thank you very much.'

Nina replaced the receiver and turned to Colin. 'Chrissie thinks Holly's mum might have gone on holiday for two weeks.'

'Two weeks!' repeated Colin.

'Where?' cried Holly again. 'Where's she gone?'

'Chrissie said they were hoping to get a last minute cheapie on the net. Somewhere in the sun.'

'*They?*' asked Colin.

'Her and her boyfriend.'

'That'll be Lenny,' said Holly miserably.

'Lenny the Louse,' said Sylvie. 'That yuck!'

'But Chrissie thinks that even if they did find a cheap flight they might not get away till tomorrow. She's offered to put a note through your mum's door on her way back from work tonight, Holly, and go round there first thing in the morning.'

Five

'She wouldn't have gone!' cried Holly, tears pricking her eyes. 'She'd have told me.'

'Not if Lenny the Louse told her not to,' put in Sylvie. 'You know she does everything he tells her.'

'She may well not have gone, Holly,' said Nina. 'We'll just have to hope that she hasn't. Come and sit down.'

Nina put her arm round her and led her to a seat. Holly saw Nina and Colin exchanging glances.

'They're wondering what to do with you now!' said Sylvie.

So was Holly. If her mum had gone on holiday she couldn't stay here with the Nightingales for two whole weeks. She hardly knew them.

'She'd have thought you'd be with your dad,' said Nina. 'It wasn't as if she was leaving you alone.'

'If they *have* gone would you have any idea where they might go?' asked Colin.

'My mum likes Majorca.'

'Have you ever been there with her?'

Holly shook her head. 'She went one time when I was staying with my dad. She said it was lovely. Another time she went to Portugal. She was going to take me to Disney. She promised. Maybe in the summer.'

Nina cleared her throat. 'So this friend, Lenny, do you know his second name?'

Holly shook her head again. When her mum had brought him home she'd just said, 'This is Lenny.'

He'd said, 'Call me Lenny the Lion!' Lenny the Louse suited him much better. People like that were dead annoying. He'd pretended to growl in her face. What an idiot! Did he think she was a baby? Her mum had laughed but Holly hadn't.

'Or where he works?' Nina went on.

'Don't know if he does.'

'When your mum goes to work,' Nina began and paused.

So here it was coming, thought Holly. The Question.

'Do you stay in the flat on your own?' Nina finished.

'I'm all right,' Holly answered quickly. 'When I go to bed I double-lock the door.' And she wasn't on her own for she had Sylvie with her. But she couldn't tell them that.

'But if you had a problem –' Nina was picking her words carefully '– is there anyone you could go to for help?'

'There's Norma across the landing. She's awful nice.'

'Does she have a phone?'

Holly nodded.

'Do you think we could phone her?'

'She won't be there. She was going to take her kids to her mum's in Birmingham for the two weeks.'

'Does she have a mobile?'

'She might do. But I've not got the number.'

Nina sighed.

'There was never any need – I just crossed the landing if I wanted her for anything,' explained Holly.

'Have another glass of wine, dear,' said Colin.

Holly hoped they weren't going to get drunk. Lenny got drunk sometimes and then he was even more horrible.

When Nina had taken a sip she was ready with her next question. 'Do you have any relatives in Glasgow? Or anywhere else? Grandparents? Aunts? Uncles?'

'I've got a granny and a grandpa.'

'Do they live in Glasgow?' asked Colin.

'They do but –'

'Great!' he said before she could finish.

'But what, Holly?' asked Nina, frowning.

'I've never seen them.'

'*Never*?'

'No.'

No one spoke for a moment, then Nina asked quietly, 'Why is that, Holly?'

Holly shrugged.

'What age is your mum?' asked Nina in the same quiet voice.

Sylvie was telling her it was none of their business but Holly didn't like not to answer. After all, she had been *dumped* on them.

'Twenty-seven,' mumbled Holly.

'So she was very young when you were born. Was that why she fell out with her mum and dad?'

'Think so.'

'You know so,' said Sylvie.

'What age is your dad?' asked Colin.

'He's two years older than my mum.'

'You've never lived with him though, not full-time?'

39

'Just for holidays. But he'd have me with him more of the time if he weren't in the oil.'

'I'm sure he would,' said Colin heartily.

'Does your dad have any parents?' asked Nina.

'He's got a mum.'

'Where is she?'

'Down south. Leeds, I think. She lives with my dad's brother. He's got a job there.'

'So you've got an uncle and another granny! Do you ever see them?'

'Not for ages. We went to visit them couple of years ago.'

'But they haven't fallen out with your dad?'

Holly shook her head. She was a bit tired of all the questions.

'Would you know their address in Leeds?'

'My dad'll have it.'

'But you haven't?'

'No.'

'Do you know what I think?' said Colin. 'That we're all tired so we should sleep on it and see what our options are in the morning. We can always email your dad if we need to.'

'A good idea.' Nina sprang up. 'I'll make you up a bed in the spare room, Holly.'

'You are remembering we've got people coming for lunch tomorrow,' said Colin to Nina.

She rolled her eyes at her husband. 'Of course… how could I forget?' she replied with a slight edge to her voice.

'I'm putting you to an awful lot of trouble.'

Nina smiled at her. 'It's no bother, we have people

staying all the time. And you're not going to sleep on the kitchen table, are you? Come with me and I'll show you where the bathroom is.'

In the Nightingales' spare room, with the poppy-patterned curtains closed, and the door shut, Holly sat up in bed wearing her new nightie with its scarlet ribbons. She was glad her mum had bought her a few new things for her stay in Edinburgh. That was the only thing she felt glad about at the moment. She could kill her mum! Going away on holiday and not telling her! With stupid old Lenny the Louse who thought he was so funny everyone should fall about laughing when he made a joke. Her mum always did. Sylvie thought that was just to keep on his right side.

'He really is a yuck!' said Sylvie. 'I don't know what she sees in him.'

'She might be in love with him?'

'Love?' scoffed Sylvie. 'With *him*?'

'What are we going to do?'

'Go to sleep. We're tired.'

When Holly woke in the morning she couldn't remember where she was. She sat bolt upright in bed and looked at the light coming through unfamiliar floral curtains.

'Where are we?'

'At the writer's of course!' replied Sylvie immediately.

'In Edinburgh. That's where she lives.'

'I want my mum!'

'Well, you can't have her right now. She's gone off with yucky Lenny the Louse.'

'She might not.'

'No, she *might* not.' Sylvie didn't sound convinced.

'I wish my dad was here.'

'You know very well he's on an oil rig in the middle of nowhere.'

He'd shown Holly a picture of an oil rig once. It was surrounded by sea. He stayed on it for weeks at a time. She'd said she didn't know how he could stick it and he'd told her it wasn't so bad, you got used to it. And it was a job. He sent money to her mum every month. She was probably using some of it to go on holiday with Lenny the Louse. Holly felt a hot surge of anger boiling up inside herself.

'I could kill her!'

'No, you couldn't,' retorted Sylvie. 'Calm down, in case the writer comes in.'

'She's called Nina.'

'I know very well what she's called. If anybody should know it would be me, wouldn't it? She's written about me often enough, hasn't she?'

'You think you know everything!'

'No, I don't. Not every single little thing.'

Holly sighed and looked up at the high ceiling. Even Sylvie was getting at her now.

'It's an awful big room for a spare.' They only had one proper bedroom and a boxroom in their Glasgow flat.

Holly slept in the boxroom. She didn't mind. It was cosy.

'It's a big house, this,' commented Sylvie.

'Kind of shabby though for a famous writer, isn't it? And messy.'

Holly had been surprised at the furniture. None of it was new. Old leather armchairs and a weird sofa thing with half a back to it, covered with fading green velvet. Nina had told her the name for it. Something French. There were bookshelves everywhere and pictures on the walls. And the stuff that was lying around! Piles of books, bundles of newspapers and magazines. Her mum would soon have half of that lot out. She liked to keep her place neat and tidy. Holly knew why. Lenny didn't like clutter. She had heard him say so.

When you've done with something chuck it! That was his motto, he said.

Sylvie said she wished Holly's mum would chuck him. Holly did too. She blamed him for taking her mum away on holiday and not letting her know where they were going. It was all his stupid stupid fault!

Holly was thumping the bedcovers with her fist when there came a tap on the door. Then it opened a crack.

'Are you awake?' asked Nina.

'Uh-huh.'

'Can I come in?'

'If you want.'

'*Say yes*,' hissed Sylvie. 'That wasn't very nice.'

It was a bit late to say anything else as Nina was already coming in. She gave Holly a smile. She wasn't dressed in smart clothes, like she was yesterday. She'd been wearing a deep blue suit with a silky yellow blouse then and she'd had her hair up. Today it was tumbling round her shoulders and she had on a pair of scuffed black corduroy trousers and a red sweatshirt. Holly was a bit disappointed. She didn't look so much like a writer now.

'Did you have a good sleep?'

'Yes, thank you.'

'That's better,' said Sylvie. 'Just remember to speak proper all the time.'

'I thought I'd just let you sleep on.' Nina went to the window and drew back the curtains. 'You must have been dead beat last night. I know I was.'

The room must look on to a garden. Holly could see treetops, some of the them frilly with pink flowers.

'What time's it?' she asked.

'Gone eleven.'

'Gone eleven!' Holly repeated. And she hadn't heard a thing!

It was dead quiet here. At home in Glasgow there was always some kind of noise going on. Traffic from the street, Norma's kids screaming through the wall, people running up and down the common stair, banging the bottom door. Holly didn't mind the noise, especially when she was in the house on her own. In fact, she quite liked it, knowing there were folk around. Norma always said she could come through to her any time she wanted but she seldom did. She preferred Sylvie to Norma's unruly kids. Sylvie said she should hope so!

'You haven't heard from Chrissie yet?' asked Holly tentatively.

'No, not yet.' Nina spoke cheerfully as if it were not a problem. 'Plenty of time.'

Nina suggested Holly might like to have a shower. 'Or a bath? Whichever you'd prefer. There are clean towels on the chair.' As she turned to go she added, 'By the way, if you hear loud boys' voices in the house that'll just be my son Johnny and his friend Tim! They'll be round shortly.'

Boys with loud voices! Neither Holly nor Sylvie fancied that.

It was while Holly was drying herself after her bath that she heard the boys arriving.

'They have got loud voices,' observed Sylvie.

'They do, don't they?' agreed Holly. She had a sick feeling at the pit of her stomach. 'I want to go home.'

'Well, you can't, can you?' said Sylvie.

'I'm just a nuisance to them.'

Sylvie could not deny that.

Holly wondered if she might have enough money in her purse for the fare back to Glasgow. Once she was dressed she checked. She did some counting in her head. Yes. She should be able to buy a train ticket and have some left over. She had a key to the flat in her bag.

'They won't let you go,' said Sylvie.

'When they're not looking we could do a runner,' said Holly.

Six

When Holly came out of the bathroom she bumped into Colin.

'I've got a couple of things to do in my study,' he said. 'Go on down and meet the boys,' he said. 'They're in the kitchen eating us out of house and home!'

They sounded like gorillas.

'You'll want some breakfast too,' Colin went on. 'I'll be down myself in a minute.'

He went into a room off the landing.

Holly lingered.

'You'd better go,' advised Sylvie. 'We'll have to wait for the right moment to make our getaway. This isn't it.'

Sylvie liked getaways. In another of Nina's books she had been tracking down a particularly nasty bunch of badger baiters and their vicious dogs and had to scarper fast. That was one of the things Holly liked about Sylvie: she had adventures. Holly never seemed to have any herself. When she watched from her window she kept hoping something good would happen in the street and she could run down and join in, and then write about it in her notebook. But it never did.

She took her time going downstairs. The kitchen door was open, just a tiny crack, but enough for sharp ears like hers to pick up snatches of conversation. She paused in the hall.

'By the way, Johnny,' Nina was in the middle of saying, 'we have a girl staying with us at the moment. It won't be for long though,' she added.

'A *girl*? Who on earth is she?'

'Someone I met at a school in Glasgow.'

'You met her in a school? You're joking.'

'I was giving a talk to her class.'

'You're always giving talks.'

'This was different.' Nina lowered her voice and Holly had to listen extra hard. 'I kind of got, well...' Nina stopped. It wasn't like her to search for the right word, thought Holly.

'Landed, you mean?'

'Never mind, she's here and that's it!'

'You didn't know her before?'

'No, I didn't.'

'So you just brought her back with you – just like that?' Johnny sounded as if he couldn't believe his ears.

'It's too complicated to go into right now. I'll explain later.'

'So what are you going to do with her?'

'Take her back to Glasgow probably.'

'So she *has* got a home to go to?'

'Well, yes, but there's a problem.'

'You're always picking up problems, Mum.'

'We haven't been able to contact her parents, that's the trouble. Not so far anyway.'

'She's a stray?'

'Don't put it like that!'

'But you can't be responsible for her, can you?'

'At the moment we are so I want you to be nice to her.' Nina's voice dropped again. 'She's not been as fortunate as you.'

Johnny grunted. 'Can't you take her back to her school?'

'It's the holidays, remember!'

'We're going up to the cottage, aren't we? You promised! Dad's taking a couple of weeks off. '

'We're going, don't worry. I need some time away too.'

'But you're not going to bring her along?'

'Of course not.'

'What will you do with her, then?'

'If we can't contact either of her parents we may have to pay a visit to the Social Services in Glasgow.'

'Did you hear that?' said Sylvie. 'You know what that means, don't you? They'll put you into care again.'

It had happened once before when Sharon had gone on holiday and then missed her plane home. Of course, it hadn't been her fault! It was the travel company. They'd changed the flight times. Somehow, Social Services had found out and Holly had been taken into care and fostered with a family. For a while it had looked as if she wouldn't be able to go back to live with her mum, but Holly had run away and gone home. So, in the end, after long conversations behind closed doors with her mum, and long conversations with Holly, the social worker in charge had let her stay. A woman called Rosemary from the Social Services still came round from time to time to see how they were getting on. She never came after nine in the evening so she didn't know about Sharon working at the *Spike*.

'Maybe now's the time to do a runner,' said Holly.

'But you've not got your stuff with you,' objected Sylvie.

'Go on in,' said Colin, coming up behind Holly and making her jump.

'Better go!' urged Sylvie. 'Get it over with. They can't eat you.'

Holly didn't feel so sure about that.

'Ah, Holly!' cried Nina as they came into the kitchen. She was standing by the cooker making toast. 'Come and meet Johnny. And his friend Tim. Boys, this is Holly.'

The boys stared at her. Holly knew straightaway which one was Johnny. He was big-built, like his dad, with a thatch of dark brown hair half falling over his eyes, but, unlike Colin, he didn't have a friendly smile. His mother had said he was thirteen but he looked older.

'Lost your voice, Johnny?' said his father.

'Hi.' Muttered Johnny, before going back to spreading peanut butter on his toast. He was ladling it on thickly. No wonder he was so big.

'Hi!' said Tim. He seemed nicer. He wasn't scowling, at least.

'Say hello,' urged Sylvie.

But Holly couldn't get the word out.

'There's a place set for you, Holly,' said Nina. 'Now what would you like for breakfast?' She spoke brightly as if she were making an extra effort.

'Not hungry.'

'I'm sure you must be,' declared Colin. 'Got to keep your strength up.'

'He's right,' said Sylvie.

'Come and sit here.' Colin indicated the seat next to him. It was at the other end of the table from Johnny.

Holly took it and Nina put a bowl of cereal in front of her. She began to eat, keeping her eyes on the spoon and the bowl.

Nina sat down too and poured herself a cup of coffee. She and Colin chatted about the weather forecast until Johnny pushed his chair back from the table and got up, announcing they had rugger practice.

He turned to his mother. 'Where did you put my kit?'

'It's in the laundry room. I haven't had time to iron it.'

'Oh, Mum!' he wailed.

'You can iron it yourself,' put in his dad. 'You're perfectly capable.'

Johnny went off grumbling. Tim thanked Nina for his breakfast before following.

'At least one of them has got some manners,' said Colin.

'Tim's mother said to me the other day what a charming boy Johnny was,' said Nina. 'Always so polite, apparently.'

She and Colin laughed.

'Typical,' said Colin. 'Charming in everybody else's house but their own.'

Holly finished her cereal, put the spoon neatly into the bowl and said, 'Thank you', in her polite voice.

Colin glanced at his watch. 'Do you know what time it is, Nina? Nearly half-past twelve.'

'For goodness sake!' She leapt up. 'It can't be!'

'It is.'

'The Smithers are coming for lunch at one! At least the ham is cooked.'

'I'll make a salad,' offered Colin.

'Colin makes interesting salads,' said his wife.

'My dad's a great cook,' said Holly.

Holly's dad always made her spaghetti Bolognese whenever she visited him. It was her favourite. He liked to have a go at different recipes. Last time they'd tried to make a chocolate cake together. It had fallen in flat in the middle and they'd had a good laugh over the whole thing. She felt a lump in her throat when she thought about it.

'What would you like to do, Holly?' asked Nina. 'Watch a DVD? Read a book? I don't think you'd want to join us for lunch. We hardly know these people. Mr Smithers has just joined Colin's medical practice as the manager.'

'He's a doctor, Colin?'

'He is. Now what's it to be?'

Holly could tell Nina was in a hurry.

'I'd like to read.'

'Come on into my study then and I'll see if I can find you something.'

Holly went with her. The room was a mess with stacks of manuscripts piled up on the floor.

'I need to do some tidying, don't I? What kind of books do you like to read?'

'I like your books.'

'That's nice to know! Writers always like to hear that.'

They studied the wall-to-wall bookshelves.

'I like those ones best.' Holly ran her fingers over them. 'They're my favourites.'

'The *Sylvie* books?'

Holly nodded.

'So you like Sylvie, do you?'

'You'd better!' said Sylvie.

'I love her books.'

'What is it you like especially about her?'

Holly shrugged. 'She just seems nice. And good fun.'

'You won't have read them all?'

'I read them over and over. But I haven't read that one.' Holly pointed.

'*Sylvie's Secret*?' Nina took it down and handed it to her. 'You can keep that copy and I'll put your name in it, if you like?'

'*Please*. Would you?'

'Of course.'

Nina found a pen on the desk and wrote beneath her name on the title page: 'To Holly, happy reading! Nina Nightingale.'

It was her second signed copy of a Nina Nightingale book. 'Thank you very much.'

Colin put his head round the door. 'Do we have any tomatoes?'

'There should be some in the fridge.'

'There aren't.'

'Are you sure?'

'I've just looked. I think we might have finished them at breakfast. I'd better pop out and get some. Anything else we need?'

'I don't know, I can't think.' Nina put a hand to her head.

'What about cream to go with the fruit salad?'

'I've got a tub.'

'Right you are then!'

Nina turned back to Holly. 'Would you be all right reading up in your bedroom?'

Holly nodded. She hugged *Sylvie's Secret* close.

'Would you like something else to eat, to take up to your room? Some fruit? A ham sandwich?'

'You won't have time, with those people coming.'

'They'll probably be late. Most people don't come on time.'

Holly opted for a ham sandwich. They went into the kitchen. Nina cut the ham in a hurry and succeeded in slicing her finger along with it.

'You're bleeding,' cried Holly.

'It's not much.' Nina sucked her finger. 'I just need a plaster, if I can find one! Johnny takes them and doesn't put them back.'

She found one in the third drawer she looked in and bound up the finger.

'I'll make my sandwich,' said Holly.

'OK, you do that. There's the bread but watch you don't cut yourself now!'

Holly watched as Nina made a dressing for Colin's salad at breakneck speed. After that she took the tub of cream out of the fridge, dumped it in a bowl and began to whisk madly.

And then it happened.

She lost control of the whisk; it jerked free of her hand, causing the bowl to tip sideways. Thick cream cascaded down into the half-open cutlery drawer.

'Oh no!' Nina gazed down into the mess.

'Oh no!' echoed Holly.

'I could scream,' wailed Nina.

But before she had the chance the doorbell rang.

'That must be your visitors,' said Holly.

'Oh no!' cried Nina again. 'And I haven't got time to change now!' She looked down at her sweat shirt, scruffy cords and trainers. 'Oh well, they'll just have to take me as I am. Let's hope they're not fussy types.'

Nina took a deep breath and went to greet her guests. Holly followed a little way into the hall to get a look at them.

Mr Smithers was wearing a grey suit and a white shirt with a plain dark blue tie. Mrs Smithers looked as if she had just emerged from the hairdresser's and been sealed all over with hairspray. She was wearing high-heeled shoes and a pale lilac suit with a velvet collar. She stood on the front doorstep eyeing her hostess's clothes. Too late, Holly noticed that some of the spilt cream had splashed over Nina's trousers.

'You are expecting us?' asked Mrs Smithers in an acid-drop voice.

'Oh yes, yes of course!' cried Nina. 'Please do come in.'

Seven

'I must apologize for my appearance,' said Nina, once she had brought the visitors in and closed the door. She shoved her hair back from her face. Holly saw that it could do with a good brush. 'We've had a bit of a problem on our hands this morning so I haven't had time to change. Colin had to pop out but he'll be back in a minute.'

Mrs Smithers murmured something that Holly couldn't make out. She was holding herself very stiffly, with her arms folded across her middle, as if she had a pain in her belly.

'Don't like the look of her,' said Sylvie.

Neither did Holly. She looked like a real pain in the neck.

'A snobby boots, too,' said Sylvie.

'Would you like to come into the sitting room and have a sherry?' invited Nina.

'We never drink alcohol in the middle of the day,' replied the woman.

'Nor would we normally. But sometimes we do when we have guests. Are you sure you won't join me?'

'Thank you, but we'd rather not.'

'I'm sure that's very sensible of you.'

Mrs Smithers uttered a little cough behind her hand. The man, Mr Smithers came and stood by her side, as stiff as a poker. He hadn't made a single sound.

'What about a glass of water then?' Nina went on. 'Orange juice? Apple juice?'

'We're fine just now.'

'Do come and have a seat in the sitting room, anyway.' Nina sounded far from fine herself. 'Make yourselves comfortable. Lunch won't be long.'

She opened the door and marched the couple in.

Holly saw her chance. 'When they're having their lunch we could make a run for it!' she suggested.

'Do you really want to go?' asked Sylvie.

'Well, we're in the way, aren't we?' It wasn't like Sylvie to miss a chance for some excitement.

'You're right. I suppose we could give it a go.'

They were both fast runners.

Nina emerged just then from the sitting room. She closed the door behind her and threw up her arms.

'She's cheesed off.' Sylvie was only stating what was evident.

'You can't blame her.' Holly replied.

'Did you hear the way the woman spoke?' Sylvie was annoyed. 'As if she'd a plum in her mouth. A sour one.'

'Holly love,' said Nina, 'do you think you could give me a hand in the kitchen?'

'You can't refuse,' said Sylvie.

Holly didn't want to refuse. She was pleased at being asked. She accompanied Nina into the kitchen.

'The first thing I must do is wash the cutlery.' Nina stared into the messy drawer. There was cream all over the floor as well. 'Do you think you could dry for me?'

'I could wash as well as dry,' offered Holly.

'Could you? If you wouldn't mind then I'll clean the floor and the drawer.'

They were in the middle of doing all that when Colin returned with the tomatoes.

'What's going on? They've arrived early!'

'I had an accident with the cream.' Nina pointed into the drawer and he came closer.

'So I can see. Have we enough left?'

'Probably not. But it'll have to do. You'd better go in and say hello to the visitors. By the way, she's ghastly!'

'Really? He's not a bad chap.'

'If he was allowed to say a word for himself, perhaps. She is awful though, isn't she, Holly?'

Holly giggled.

Colin strode off to the sitting room and Nina and Holly carried on with their chores, after which they set out the cutlery. Holly was given paper napkins, which she folded into neat shapes while Nina arranged the food on the table.

Colin popped his head round the door and asked if he could bring the guests through yet.

'I suppose you'd better.' Nina made a face.

'I see what you mean about her.'

He went out to return a moment later with Mr and Mrs Smithers.

'I hope you don't mind eating in the kitchen?' said Nina.

'You can see she does mind,' commented Sylvie. 'She's a right snoot.'

'We like to be fairly casual for lunch,' said Nina to the

Smithers. She turned to Holly. 'That's been a great help. If you want to go, Holly, that's fine.'

Holly took her ham sandwich and left them to it.

Up in the bedroom Sylvie suggested that this would be the time to go if they were going. 'If you *really* want to.'

Holly had mixed feelings. If she did stay they'd end up taking her to the Social Services in Glasgow. They'd said so, hadn't they? But if she and Sylvie went home to the flat in Glasgow the Social Services would track them down there anyway.

'Where else could we go, Sylvie?'

'Don't worry. We'd find somewhere.' Sylvie sounded confident. She was always ready for anything. 'It'll be an adventure. You've been wanting to have an adventure, haven't you? Stop dithering then!'

Quickly, Holly packed her nightdress, *Sylvie's Secret* and the ham sandwich in her pink bag. The writer had said she could keep the book so it wouldn't be a case of nicking it. It was *hers*.

She pulled on her jacket and crept out on to the landing where she paused to listen to the voices rising up from the kitchen. Nina's and Colin's voices. The visitors didn't seem to be saying much, if anything. Colin laughed. Then Nina laughed. The visitors weren't laughing.

'They probably don't know how to,' said Sylvie.

'Let's go!' said Holly.

She tiptoed down the stairs, Sylvie with her all the way. It was good to know that Sylvie was always there and she was never on her own, especially at a time like this, on the brink of an adventure. Suddenly she hit a creaky stair and stood stock still for a minute but Holly didn't think they could have heard down in the kitchen, not with Nina and Colin talking at the tops of their voices. They'd be hoarse by the time they got rid of those people.

In the bottom hall Holly stopped again.

'Do have some more ham,' Nina was saying.

The only response was a murmur.

'They'll be turning it down,' said Holly.

'Very likely,' agreed Sylvie. '*We don't have seconds*,' she mimicked Mrs Smithers, and Holly smiled.

'Salad?' That was Colin. 'More bread? Oatcakes? How about some cheese?'

'We'd better get our skates on,' said Sylvie. 'They might not want much more lunch.'

A few more steps, and they had reached the front door.

'Open it quietly now,' Sylvie cautioned. 'And don't bang it behind us. You know your mum's always telling you off for banging the door.'

The front door was quite heavy but Holly opened it carefully, scarcely daring to breathe.

'Ready?' asked Sylvie. They'd have to run like the clappers.

'Ready,' replied Holly.

She stepped outside and eased the door shut behind them. It had made scarcely a sound. Then she turned and took off like a rocket.

And collided with Johnny heading up the path on his bike.

They ended up in a heap on the ground, tangled together amongst the spinning bicycle wheels. Johnny glared at her over the top of them.

'What did you think you were doing?' he bellowed. 'Coming barging out the door like that?'

'I didn't see you.'

'This is my new bike. Look at it, you've scratched it!'

'I couldn't help it!'

'If you'd looked where you were going –'

'You don't have to shout,' Holly shouted back.

She couldn't get up. His stupid machine was lying on top of her, trapping her leg, and he was making no effort to help her up.

'Kick him,' advised Sylvie, but Holly couldn't get a foot free. She was trying to get her breath back. She'd banged her elbow too. Surely Johnny was holding the bike down on her deliberately.

'Let me up!' screamed Holly. 'You're hurtin' me.'

'Why were you running away? What have you got in that bag?' He yanked it out of her hand and dangled it high above her head.

'Give it back to me! I've not stole nothing. Let me up! You're hurting me.'

The front door opened suddenly behind them.

'What in the name of goodness is going on?' demanded Colin.

'Dad,' yelled Johnny, leaping to his feet, 'she was running off. And I don't know what she's got in this bag!' He held it out.

'I've not stole nothing,' repeated Holly angrily,

finally managing to shove the bike aside before scrambling up.

'I'll bet she has! Why else would she be running away?'

'Run for it now,' advised Sylvie, but they both knew they'd never make it. Johnny could easily trip them up before they'd got as far as the gate. He looked mean enough.

Nina appeared at the door now. 'What's going on?'

Holly wished they'd stop asking that. They were doing her head in.

'Let's go inside,' said Colin. 'And, Johnny, please give Holly her bag back. I am sure she has stolen nothing. Also, apologize to her!'

Johnny glared at his father, then shrugged and thrust the bag into Holly's hands.

'Johnny!' growled his father in a fierce voice.

'Sorry,' muttered Johnny.

Holly couldn't help feeling pleased but she knew this was trouble. He'd hate her for it.

'That's one in the eye for him at any rate,' murmured Sylvie.

'And pick your bike up, please, Johnny,' said Colin. 'We don't want it left lying in the middle of the path where someone might fall over it.'

Like the visitors, thought Holly. Though that could be a laugh, as Sylvie pointed out. It might dent the woman's puffball hair.

Johnny did as he was told, though he didn't stop scowling.

Once they were inside he went galloping ahead and

raced up the stairs, taking two and three steps at a time. They heard him slam the door of his room shut.

'In the huff,' said Sylvie. 'You've made an enemy there for sure.'

Holly didn't need Sylvie to point that out.

'Now then,' started Nina, 'I think we need to have a little talk, Holly. *Were* you trying to run away?'

'Don't forget the Smithers,' Colin reminded her in a hushed voice.

'How could I?' she replied equally quietly, glancing over her shoulder. 'But I think this is rather more important. You go back and join them and make my apologies. I'll take Holly into my study.'

At that moment the kitchen door opened and the visitors emerged.

'We can see you are otherwise engaged,' said Mrs Smithers as she came mincing towards them. 'So we thought we would just take our leave now.'

'But you haven't had your pudding,' cried Colin.

'We never eat dessert,' said Mrs Smithers.

She looked as if she didn't ever eat anything much at all. Now that Holly had a proper close-up view of her, she saw that Mrs Smithers was as thin as a pin. A sharp one. She was eyeing Holly in return with a beady eye.

'I'm really terribly sorry,' said Nina helplessly. 'Just circumstances, you know…' Her voice trailed away.

'We're circumstances now,' observed Sylvie. 'Did you get that? Writers like to say things in different ways.'

'You must come another time.' Colin was making an

effort to sound cheery but not doing it terribly well. 'And we'll make up for today.'

'Not if Nina has any say in it they won't,' said Sylvie.

From the look on Nina's face Holly could see that she wanted the Smithers to walk out through the front door as quickly as possible and never come back.

'Thank you very much for a nice lunch,' said Mr Smithers, shaking hands with Nina and then Colin. He seemed a polite man at least.

'Thank you,' bleated his wife, who also offered a hand, a droopy one.

'Apologies once again,' said Colin with a little bow, as he showed the visitors out.

The door closed behind them.

'What an absolute, total, utter disaster!' declared Nina.

'And it's all our fault,' said Sylvie.

Eight

There was silence for a moment and then Nina giggled. She couldn't hold it back. So Holly giggled too. And Colin began to laugh. They were all laughing so much that Johnny came out of his room and glared down on them from the top landing.

'What are you laughing about?'

'Those dreadful people,' cried Nina, wiping her eyes.

'He's not so bad,' rejoined Colin. 'Just a bit of a bore.'

Nina started to laugh again.

'What's the joke?' demanded Johnny. 'Who are you talking about?'

'Tell you later,' said his father.

'He doesn't like feeling he's left out,' said Sylvie.

Holly could understand that but, this time, it was nothing to do with her, thank goodness.

The telephone rang and Holly's heart jumped. Could it be Chrissie with news of her mum? Colin went ahead of them into the kitchen and lifted the receiver.

'Oh, hello, it's Chrissie, is it?'

Holly positioned herself close to Colin.

'No, that's fine. I understand you wouldn't have been able to go round too early.' He listened. 'The flat seemed to be empty? No answer when you rang the bell?'

Holly's hopes plummeted.

'Would you like to have a word with my wife?' Colin passed the receiver over to Nina.

Chrissie was sorry she couldn't be of any further help. She had rung the bell several times. She had no idea where Sharon might have gone.

'Thanks very much, anyway, for trying,' said Nina and she hung up the phone. There was a long silence, during which Holly saw Nina and Colin's eyes meet.

'We could try sending an email to my dad,' suggested Holly.

'Do you have his email address?'

'I could get it from my mum's. I always go with her to the library and help her do it. I know the password.'

'Come on then, let's give it a go!'

Holly followed Nina into her study and they sat down together in front of the computer. Nina opened up the internet and then let Holly take over.

She typed in her mum's address and password. The account came up.

'There's one new message.' Holly opened it. 'It's from my dad!'

'Can you read it to me?'

'Dear Sharon and Holly, I am very sorry but I am going to have to postpone my leave for two weeks. I feel awful about this but I have no choice. Something urgent has come up and they need me. I hope it won't be a problem for you. Looking forward very much to seeing you Holly, pet. Love, Dad.'

'Well!' declared Nina, sitting back in her chair.

Two weeks, Holly was thinking. Her dad really wouldn't be here for *two weeks*. What was she going to do?

'Your mum hadn't opened that message, had she?' said Nina.

'No.'

'When did he send it?' Nina craned her next to look. 'Ten, no, twelve days ago. Your mum mustn't check her email very regularly.'

'No, she doesn't. She can't really be bothered.'

'Right then, let's reply to your dad. Would you like me to write it?'

Holly gave way.

Nina explained as briefly as she could who she was and how Holly had come to be staying with her and her husband. She then put down their landline and mobile phone numbers and asked Holly's dad to call as soon as he received the message.

'He doesn't always get them straightaway,' said Holly. 'Depends what he's doing.'

'I expect it does.'

They returned to the kitchen and Nina broke the news to Colin.

'Two weeks,' he echoed.

'They don't know what they're going to do about you, Holly,' murmured Sylvie.

'You don't have to go on about it!' Holly snapped back.

The door opened and Johnny put his head round. 'Mum…'

'Hang on a minute, Johnny,' said his mother. 'We need to have a little chat with Holly on her own.'

He backed out, looking sulky.

'We won't be long,' his father called after him.

'Now then, Holly,' began Nina, 'first of all we need to get something sorted out. Colin says it looked like you were about to run away? Is that true?'

Holly lowered her head and examined the state of her nails.

'You must stop biting them,' scolded Sylvie.

'You were, weren't you?' pressed Nina.

'Might.'

'Where were you going to go?'

'Glasgow.'

'Have you got a key to your flat?'

'Uh-huh. I've got money too. Some that my mum gave me for spending. And there's plenty tins in the house.'

'You couldn't stay there on your own.'

'Yes, I could!' Holly looked up. 'I can manage.'

'That's as maybe. But you're too young, dear. You're not allowed to stay alone at your age. It's against the law.'

'People don't need to know,' Holly mumbled. 'Not if nobody tells them.'

'We would have to, I'm afraid. We couldn't possibly let you do it.'

'We'd worry about you,' Colin added.

'You wouldn't need to. I'd be real careful, honest I would. I always put the gas off on the cooker and I don't open the door to nobody I don't know. My mum had a peephole put in so that I can see who's there.'

'Even so...' Nina's voice tailed away. She sounded weary. Those slithery Smithers must have exhausted her. 'We'll just have to wait till your dad gets the email and calls, then see what he has to say.'

'Your grandmother in Leeds might be able to come up and fetch you,' suggested Colin.

Holly doubted that. Granny Hamilton had a bad back and seemed to spend half the time in bed.

Johnny put his head round the door again. 'Mum... You're remembering Tim's coming for a sleepover. He's coming round at three.'

'That's early for a sleepover!'

'His mum and dad are going away for the night.'

The front door bell rang.

'That'll be him now,' Johnny vanished.

'We must go shopping, Colin,' said Nina. 'Do you want to come, Holly, or would you be all right on your own? Colin and the boys will be here.'

Holly couldn't help herself. 'I feel horrible,' she burst out. 'I'm just a bother to you.'

'You are nothing of the kind!' said Colin.

'You're only saying that. You don't really want me here.' Why should they?

'We are very happy to have you in our house.'

'We *are*!' agreed Nina. 'It's not a problem.'

'Are you sure?' Holly asked.

'She's already said it was a problem,' Sylvie reminded Holly. 'Remember? To the Smithereens.' Sylvie was pleased that she'd thought up the word. When Holly wrote up her notes about the visitors that would be what she'd call those dreadful people.

'In the meantime, Holly,' Nina went on, 'you must promise that you will not try to run away again!'

'Promise!' ordered Sylvie.

'Promise,' muttered Holly.

'Now why don't you go upstairs and take your coat off, love? And then come back down and have some lunch. We've still got loads of ham and salad left and you've only had a sandwich. All right?'

'All right.'

Holly took her bag and left the room, passing the two boys who were on their way down the stairs. Johnny didn't even glance at her though Tim gave her a quick grin.

As the boys reached the bottom hall Holly heard Johnny say, 'Is *she* staying?'

'Her name is Holly,' his mother responded. 'And keep your voice down.'

'Well, is she?'

'For the present, yes.'

The kitchen door closed.

Holly took off her coat and hovered on the top landing. She was hungry but didn't feel like going down to join those two horrors.

She wanted her mum.

'Well, she's not here,' chided Sylvie. 'No point in greeting or going on about it. She'll come back when she's ready.'

Holly still did not move.

'You can't just stand here sulking. Give yourself a wash. Then go on down. Nina and Colin will be expecting you.'

They welcomed Holly back into the kitchen and Nina told her to help herself to whatever she fancied. Johnny and Tim were already at the table eating.

'What are we going to do about my bike?' asked Johnny. 'The paintwork's all scratched.'

'Nothing that a lick of paint won't sort,' responded his father. 'Didn't look serious to me.'

'I hurt my wrist too. I think I might have sprained it.'

'I doubt it.' His father didn't seem to be impressed by that either. 'You look as if you're using it well enough at the moment.'

'Let's give the subject a rest, *please*!' demanded his mother. 'We don't want to hear any more about it. It was an accident.'

Johnny mumbled something.

'And don't talk with your mouth full!'

Johnny glowered.

As soon as lunch was over he was off with Tim.

'Where are you going?' his mother called after him.

'Out.' He was away.

Nina shook her head. 'He's so moody these days.'

'He's thirteen,' returned his father. 'It's not uncommon.'

'He wants everything his own way.'

'He has to learn he can't have it.'

'He doesn't like you being here either of course,' said Sylvie to Holly.

'I think I'd better get moving.' Nina glanced at her watch. 'Time's going on.'

She got up. 'Are you sure you don't want to come with me, Holly?'

'No, I'll be fine.'

'I'll be in my study if you need me,' said Colin.

It was peaceful if messy in the kitchen after everyone had gone. After Holly had eaten she set to and cleared the place up. Her mum would have been proud of her. She kept looking hopefully at the phone but it didn't ring.

It was almost six o'clock before Nina returned laden with shopping.

'Gosh, you've cleared up, Holly!' cried Nina. 'You didn't have to do that.'

'I didn't mind. I usually clear up after my mum goes to work.'

The phone rang while Nina was cooking dinner. Holly froze. The caller turned out to be a friend of Nina's.

When the boys came back Johnny announced they were starving so Nina fed them first and let them go, which pleased Holly.

'It'll be getting on for midnight in the Middle East,' said Colin, when the three of them, finally, sat down to eat. 'I don't think we can expect your dad to call before tomorrow now, Holly.'

Nine

Holly had breakfast with Nina and Colin. Poached eggs on toast. She usually just had a bowl of cornflakes by herself. Her mum worked late so slept late.

There was no sign of the boys.

'They'd sleep till Doomsday if you let them,' said Nina.

'They're growing lads,' said Colin. 'Do you like to sleep in, Holly?'

'Not really.'

As they were clearing up, the doorbell rang. For one wild moment Holly thought it might be her mum come to call for her.

'How would she know where you were?' demanded Sylvie.

Colin went to see who it was.

'Early for a Sunday morning,' commented Nina.

The caller turned out to be Tim's dad, who had arrived to collect his son. They were going to visit relatives in Fife. After Nina introduced Holly, she and Tim's dad chatted while Colin went to rouse Tim.

Holly got up and went to stand by the window. She looked into the fresh green garden with its spring flowers making pretty splashes of colour here and there. Their back green in Glasgow was only a scabby bit of grass where you could hang your clothes out if you wanted to. Her mum had stopped putting theirs out after her best silk top and a new pair of jeans had been nicked from the line. Mrs Blackie, who lived in the next stair and was a pain in the neck, had said only an idiot would hang their clothes outside these days. When she was young you could leave them out all week and nobody would touch them. She was constantly on the watch for troublemakers of all kinds. She loved reporting people to the police or the council. For putting their rubbish out the night before instead of the morning. Dropping litter. Letting their dogs mess the pavement. She was kept busy.

Tim came rocketing into the room looking half asleep, with his hair tousled and the laces of his trainers undone.

'Steady!' cautioned his dad. 'Not sure you can go visiting looking like that. Your mother might have something to say.'

Holly saw Nina smile.

'Trouble is,' said Sylvie, after Tim and his dad had departed, 'we're not used to boys barging about making a racket.'

The phone rang and Holly's hopes soared again.

It was Mike for Johnny.

'He'll call you back,' said Nina.

She then marched purposefully up the stairs and told Johnny to get up – now! He came down a few minutes later, yawning, still in his pyjamas.

'We thought we might take a run down the coast,' said his mother 'and have lunch out. Want to come?'

He didn't. He'd go and see Mike instead.

They went to a cosy restaurant by the sea and had a nice lunch. Nina and Colin chose roast beef and Holly had fish and chips. Her favourite. She wasn't used to so many big meals but found she was enjoying them. Quite often she and her mum would have beans on toast or something simple although when Lenny came he'd bring a carryout of fish and chips or pizza.

Colin's mobile rang in the middle of lunch. Holly put down her knife and fork.

It was Johnny. He'd forgotten his key. Holly sighed.

'Well, you'll just have to go back to Mike's,' his dad was saying.

'I suspect he's lost it.' His mother shook her head. '*Again.*'

It had rained on the way but by the time they left the restaurant the sun had come out. Nina suggested a walk along the beach. Then she looked down at Holly's black patent shoes and decided they'd better keep to the path.

The sea sparkled in the sunshine and a group of boys played volleyball on the sand.

They had walked only a little way when Colin's phone went again.

'Probably not him,' Sylvie warned Holly.

They stopped while Colin took the call.

'Sorry.' He frowned. 'I can't hear you, I'm sorry. It's a bad line.' He listened, clicked it off and shrugged. 'Couldn't make anything out.'

'It might have been my dad,' cried Holly. She was beside herself.

'If it was I'm sure he'll try again,' said Nina.

They moved on. They'd walked for quite a while before the phone rang for the third time.

'Take it in the lee of the building, Colin,' advised Nina. 'Out of the wind.'

He moved towards the wall. Holly crossed both sets of fingers behind her back.

'Who's calling, please?' Colin bent his head as he tried to hear. 'Can you speak up? Joe?'

'Joe Hamilton,' shrieked Holly. 'That's my dad.'

'Hang on,' said Colin and he started to walk rapidly away from the beach and the sound of the sea to an alleyway across the road, with Holly and Nina running behind him. 'That's better. Can you hear me now? I'm Colin Nightingale. You must have got my wife's email?' He was still having to shout. After a moment or two he turned. 'Your dad wants to speak to you, Holly.'

Her hand trembled as she took the phone.

'Dad?'

'Aye, it's me, Holly love. How're you doin'?'

'All right. Are you coming home?'

'I'm afraid I can't, pet, not right now, I'm really sorry.' He sounded upset. 'We've hit a serious problem, you see, and they need me.'

'You need him too,' said Sylvie.

'What am I going to do?'

'These folk you're with? Are they OK?'

'They are, Dad, they are! Nina writes books and Colin's a doctor.'

'So they can take care of you.'

'But I can't stay with them, not for two whole weeks.'

'I wasne suggesting that. I meant for just now.'

'What *is* he suggesting then?' put in Sylvie.

'Have you any idea where your mum's gone?'

'Might be Majorca.'

He swore, then said, 'Don't worry, pet, I'll fix something up.'

There was a noise on the line as if the sea had come between them.

'Dad!' shouted Holly.

The noise cleared and his voice came back. 'Tell you what, I'll phone my pal Ricky and ask him if he and his wife Brenda could have you. You know them. You like them, don't you?'

'They're OK.'

She didn't like them that much but it would be better than being taken to the Social Services and put into care. Better than not being allowed to go back to her mum afterwards because they'd say she wasn't fit to look after her. But she was! Holly was sure it had been that spiteful Mrs Blackie who had clyped on her mum before.

'I'll ring you back later,' said her dad and the line went dead.

'He's going to sort it out.' Holly told Nina and Colin about her dad's pal Ricky.

'Great,' said Nina. 'I think we'll walk back now and head for home.'

There were a lot of cars on the road with people returning to town after spending Sunday by the sea.

The traffic gradually began to slow until they were brought to a full stop. They could see cars stretching all the way along the road in front of them until they were out of sight.

'It's not usually this bad.' Holly could see Colin frowning in the mirror. 'I hope it's not an accident.'

His mobile rang.

It was Johnny to ask if he could stay the night at Mike's. They were going to have an impromptu party. Just a few of them. Could he go?

'Say yes,' whispered Nina.

After ten minutes had passed, during which time they hadn't moved at all, Colin found a local station on the radio.

'Here we are, traffic report!' He turned up the volume.

He was right: there had been an accident about half a mile further up the road, which was now completely blocked. The reporter said that police and ambulances were on their way to the scene.

'I'd better see if I can go and help.'

Colin pulled the car over and parked on the verge. Then he jumped out and went round to the boot to take out a First Aid box. He sprinted off up the road, weaving his way around the parked cars.

'I hope it's not a bad accident,' said Holly.

'So do I,' agreed Nina. 'Climb over to the front, dear. It'll be easier for us to talk that way.'

They chatted about books and Holly's school and Nina told her about places in the world she'd visited. They didn't speak about the accident.

It was over an hour before Collin came back.

'How was it?' asked Nina.

He made a face. 'They've got an ambulance through and they're taking them to hospital. I think you'd better drive.' Holly saw that he had blood on his hands. 'Not that we'll get away yet. They're waiting for a tow truck to clear the road.'

Nina suddenly remembered something. Holly could tell that she had, the way her head jerked up.

'I'd totally forgotten,' she began.

'Forgotten what?' asked Colin.

'We're due at the Mannings' for dinner this evening.'

'The *Mannings*?'

'Yes, you know the Mannings. John and Evangeline.'

'Of course I know them! First I heard about going out to dinner tonight.'

'I told you several days ago.'

'I don't remember.'

'Well, I did.'

Silence for a moment, then Colin asked, 'What time are we due?'

'Seven thirty for eight.'

'What time is it now?'

They all examined their watches, even Holly. Her dad had given her a pretty one with flowers on the face and a pink wristband for her birthday. He always gave her nice presents. So did her mum.

'Half-past six,' groaned Colin. 'We'll be lucky even to be home by half-past seven.'

'I'll ring and warn them we might be late.' Nina

78

stopped and looked round at Holly.

'I'll be all right,' jumped in Holly. 'You needn't worry about me.'

The house was big but she could stay in her room and read and she'd have Sylvie with her for company. It'd be like when she was at home and her mum was at work.

'It's out of the question, Holly. We can't possibly leave you on your own. We wouldn't even consider it.'

Holly had been afraid of that.

They were quiet now. Holly could see only the backs of their heads.

'They're wondering what to do about you,' said Sylvie.

'And not for the first time,' replied Holly.

Ten

The traffic still wasn't moving.

'What about that girl who used to babysit for us?' said Colin. 'The one who played football in the back garden with Johnny?'

'You mean Abigail? She's in her second year at university. In Manchester.'

'I am a bit behind the times! Anybody else you can think of? We haven't needed a babysitter for a while, have we? Johnny always seems to be able to go to a pal.'

'How could I ask anyone now?' demanded Nina. 'At the very last minute?'

'I suppose somebody might be free and be glad to make a few quid. We could pay double.'

Holly was appalled. 'I don't want you to have to pay money for me!'

'Don't worry about it, Holly,' said Colin.

But she was worrying.

'We *are* a complication,' sighed Sylvie.

'Better call Evangeline,' said Colin wearily.

Nina scrabbled in her bag and found her mobile. Her call was answered straightaway.

'Evangeline,' she started, 'we've got a problem. I'm really terribly sorry but I don't think we'll be able to come tonight –'

She broke off as Evangeline must have cut in.

'No, listen,' continued Nina, but Evangeline didn't seem to want to. Nina looked at Colin and rolled her eyes.

'She must be a right gasbag,' remarked Sylvie.

Holly would have loved to have been able to hear what the woman was saying.

'Nosy parker!' chanted Sylvie.

Holly didn't deny it. She was interested in people. Just like Nina.

'We are actually on the road at the moment. Yes, on the road,' shouted Nina. 'What are we doing here? Coming back from the coast.'

She covered the mobile with her hand and said to Colin, 'The connection's terrible. All I can make out is Evangeline rattling on and on. Though she's obviously picked up the message that we might not be able to come to dinner.'

'I don't suppose she's pleased.'

'Hardly!' Nina went back to the call. 'We're caught in a traffic jam. There's been an accident… No, *we* haven't been in an accident. I'll call you when we get home. The traffic's beginning to move.'

Nina flipped her phone closed and started the engine. That was the end of Evangeline for the moment.

They crept slowly forward, stopping and starting at intervals. The traffic was only moving in one direction at a time. They reached the accident spot where a crumpled car lay on its side.

'Will they survive?' Nina asked Colin.

'Think so. They've got a good chance anyway.'

'It was good that Colin was able to go and help, wasn't it?' said Sylvie.

Holly thought so too.

The police waved them through and after another few miles they began to speed up.

Holly was glad when they arrived in Edinburgh. It was after seven o'clock and she needed to go to the loo. They'd been in the car for hours.

She washed her hands and combed her fingers through her hair then went downstairs to rejoin Nina and Colin. The kitchen door was ajar and Nina was talking on the phone. Holly hesitated.

'I can't go into it just now,' Nina was saying, 'except to tell you that we are looking after a young girl I met at a school in Glasgow. Her father is working abroad –' There was a pause. 'No, I know I haven't mentioned her before… I only met her on Friday… Why are we looking after her? She needs our help, that's why. Look, I'll see what I can do, Evangeline, that's all I can promise. We're just in. I'll phone you back.'

'I guess you're not too popular with Evangeline?' said Colin.

'Evangeline just will not listen!' Nina sounded at the end of her tether.

'She suffers from verbal diarrhoea, that's her problem.'

'Nobody's pleased of course when you cancel for a dinner party. Especially at the last minute. I understand that. I don't like doing it. I wouldn't do it unless it was absolutely necessary.'

'I feel awful,' moaned Holly under her breath.

'You can't help it,' returned Sylvie.

'Let's sit down and consider our options,' said Colin.

'Finding a babysitter at this time of night is totally out.'

'We could get Johnny to come home?'

'Oh no!' thought Holly.

'That wouldn't work,' said Nina. Holly breathed a sigh of relief. 'We can't leave Holly on her own.'

'Agreed.'

'So…what about you going to the Mannings on your own, Colin?'

'*Me*?'

'Yes, why not?'

'Why don't you go and I'll look after Holly?'

'She'd probably feel easier with me. This whole business might be disruptive for us but it must be quite traumatic for her, let's remember that. Her dad not turning up. Having to stay with strangers. She's coping very well.'

'She does seem to accept whatever's thrown at her.'

'I suspect that's been the story of her life. Shunted here and there.'

Holly wriggled uncomfortably.

'What if neither of us were to go?' That was Colin's idea and Sylvie thought it a good one. 'I've never enjoyed their parties anyway.'

'One of us will have to go. Evangeline would have a heart attack if we didn't.'

'Might be a good idea, her having a heart attack.'

'Now, Colin!'

'Well, it would stop her having dinner parties, wouldn't it?'

Holly giggled quietly.

There was a lull. They must have run out of ideas. And then the phone rang.

'You go, Colin,' said Nina. 'You're nearer.'

'It might be my dad!' cried Holly, forgetting that she was trying to remain hidden.

'Or Evangeline,' added Sylvie.

Holly pushed the door open a little way.

Colin was talking. 'I see. Yes, I understand.' Turning he saw Holly and said, 'Just a moment, dear.' He held up his hand.

Holly retreated and the door closed behind her.

'I think it must be your dad,' said Sylvie.

Holly couldn't make out what was being said now. She had the feeling that Colin might be keeping his voice down so that she couldn't hear. It seemed like ages before Nina came out and said her dad wanted to speak to her.

Holly dashed into the kitchen and took the receiver from Colin. The line was clearer this time.

'Hello, Dad.'

'How're you doin', pet?'

'Fine. I'm fine.'

'Good. Listen, love, I couldn't get hold of Ricky.'

'Oh no!'

'I rang his mum and she said they'd gone on holiday.' Everyone was on holiday, Holly thought. Except her.

'So what am I going to do?'

'Dr Nightingale has very kindly offered to let you stay on with them.'

'For two *weeks*?'

'I know, it's good of them. But you do like them, don't you?'

'Yes, of course. But –' Holly looked over at Nina and Colin, both of whom gave her reassuring smiles.

Her dad was talking again. 'Dr Nightingale tells me he's a GP. He's given me the name of a doctor at the Infirmary in Edinburgh. As a reference. I think I can trust him..?'

'Oh, you can but – !'

'I don't know what else to do, Holly.' Her dad sounded miserable.

'You don't want to go into care,' murmured Sylvie.

'Will you be all right, love? Staying with them?'

'Yes,' said Holly slowly. 'I'll be all right.'

She stood still for a moment after she'd put the phone down. Then she turned to face Nina and Colin.

'Are you sure?'

'We are,' said Nina. 'Absolutely sure. We discussed it earlier. We are happy to have you stay with us.'

'Thanks very much,' said Holly limply. What else could she say?

'That's that settled then!' declared Colin. 'Now back to Evangeline.'

Nina groaned. 'She says she set the date specifically to suit us. That's rubbish! She's got friends from America staying who are apparently dying to meet me.' Nina didn't sound as if she was dying to meet them. 'The woman has got an absolutely brilliant idea for a children's book and would love to discuss it with me! She thinks it could be as big as Harry Potter.'

'Gosh!' exclaimed Holly.

'A lot of people think writing for children is easy, Holly. I've been sent a few manuscripts in my time. Usually they can't write for toffee.'

'I can see why you don't want to go,' said Colin and sighed theatrically. 'I feel I am about to be sacrificed.'

Holly laughed.

'She's a good cook,' Nina reminded him.

'I'm not that hungry.'

Nina gave Colin a look, and rang Evangeline. She spoke very decisively. 'Colin will be with you in fifteen minutes but I'm terribly sorry I won't be able to make it. I simply have to stay with Holly.'

☆   ☆   ☆

Nina and Holly had a quiet meal together in the kitchen.

'It's going to be something simple,' announced Nina. 'Like bacon and eggs?'

'I like bacon and eggs.'

'Good! That's what we'll have then. I'll put the bacon on to grill and you can set the table. I think you know where the cutlery is now, and you'll find some serviettes in the cupboard.'

Holly laid the table carefully, making sure the knives and forks were lined up correctly and when the food was ready they sat down to eat together.

'I feel awful,' said Holly, 'about you not getting to your dinner.'

'Don't! To be honest, I wasn't fussy about going.'

'Why? Don't you like your friend?'

'She's all right.'

'But she's not your best friend?'

'No, she's definitely not my best friend. Have you got a best friend?'

'I've got a couple of pals at school,' said Holly awkwardly, not looking Nina in the eye. She didn't have anyone special really, except for Sylvie, and she couldn't tell Nina about her.

'Good pals?'

Holly shrugged.

'Do you see them out of school?'

'Not much. They don't live very near. And Lenny doesn't like us having people in.'

'So whatever Lenny says goes?'

'Sort of.'

'Not just sort of!' scoffed Sylvie. 'Your mum's daft. She lets him boss her around.'

'Do you like school?'

'It's OK. I've got a nice teacher.'

Holly didn't really mind Nina asking her questions now. She understood that writers might want to know things. She did herself after all.

'How are you getting on with *Sylvie's Secret*?' asked Nina.

Holly started to talk about the book and before she knew it she was telling Nina all about the people in it and what was happening.

'She knows all that,' Sylvie reminded her. 'Don't forgot she wrote it!'

'What is it you like so much about Sylvie?'

'She does all sorts of interesting things and she doesn't let anything stop her. And she's got lots of friends. She's really nice.'

'I'm glad you think so, Holly.'

'Oh, I do. I really do!'

'Is she the kind of friend you'd like to have?'

Holly nodded. Then she wondered if Nina had overheard her talking to Sylvie for sometimes she did talk out loud. She blushed at the thought.

Nina paused and cocked her head. 'Did you hear something? Sounds like the front door.'

She got up and went to see. Holly followed. Maybe Colin couldn't stand the dinner party and had walked out.

'Johnny!' cried Nina. 'What are you doing back here? I thought you were staying the night at Mike's?'

'He was sick so they had to cancel the party.'

'Oh, dear, what a shame! Poor Mike.'

It was a shame, thought Holly. She'd been having a really nice time, chatting away about this and that to Nina, until Johnny had come butting in.

'It is his home,' murmured Sylvie.

He suddenly noticed her.

'Holly's going to be staying on with us for a couple of weeks,' explained Nina.

He gaped. 'But aren't we going up to the cottage for the holidays?'

'We are. Tomorrow.'

Johnny kept on staring at Holly. She looked away. She'd just got used to being here in this house, she didn't feel like going somewhere new.

'I was going to ask if Tim could come with us,' said Johnny. 'In fact, I've already asked him and his mother has said he can go.'

'Well, I'm afraid you'll just have to un-ask him then. You should have consulted me first.'

Was there such a word as un-ask? Sylvie asked Holly, who thought maybe the writer had made it up. She supposed writers might do that sometimes.

'I can't put him off now!' yelled Johnny.

'No need to shout! I'm not deaf. *I'll* have a word with Tim's mother. I'm sure she'll understand.'

'But will Tim?' said Sylvie.

'I want Tim to come!' Johnny wasn't backing down yet.

'We'll talk about it later,' said his mother. 'Knowing you, I expect you'd like something to eat?'

'I think I'll go to bed,' said Holly and slid off up the stairs.

She closed her bedroom door firmly. She didn't want to eavesdrop this time and hear what Johnny was saying to his mother. The only words she'd caught as she was leaving were, 'It's not fair!'

Eleven

The telephone rang while they were having breakfast, the three of them, Nina, Colin and Holly. There was no sign yet of Johnny.

'Who can that be at this time of the morning?' growled Colin. 'It never stops. We can't even eat our breakfast in peace.'

'I'll get it.' Nina lifted the receiver. 'Oh, Evangeline!' Her voice dropped as she said the woman's name.

She didn't get a chance to say anything more as Evangeline was already gabbing on at the other end. Holly wondered why Nina hadn't told her to get lost ages ago.

'This *morning*?' said Nina, when there was a pause. 'No, I'm afraid I couldn't. We're going up to the cottage –'

Another volley of words came issuing forth at the other end, during which Nina covered the mouthpiece with her hand and said in a loud whisper to Colin, 'She wants to bring that American woman over.'

'When?'

'Now.'

'Out of the question.'

'I know that.'

'Stand firm!'

'Don't worry!' retorted Nina, who had tried to cut across Evangeline a couple of times, without success.

Colin passed Holly a glass of orange juice.

Nina was still listening, and frowning. She covered the receiver again and turned back to them. 'Would you believe it, the woman wants me to co-author her stupid book with her!'

'Write it, you mean,' returned Colin. 'She suffers from the same verbal diarrhoea as Evangeline. I had to sit beside her for dinner. You don't know how lucky you were to escape!'

Nina was getting really annoyed now. When at last she did manage to get her oar in she said loudly and firmly, 'Evangeline, I'm sorry but I am not interested in co-authoring anything with anybody. I like to write books on my own. Do apologize to your friend that I am unable to see her but we are about to pack and go!' With that, she slammed the receiver back into its slot so abruptly that it bounced back out and had to be replaced. 'What a nerve!'

Holly thought so too. Maybe they wouldn't get asked to dinner at Evangeline's again. If she were them, she'd be pleased about that.

'I can't wait to get away,' said Nina when she sat down again to her breakfast. Her boiled egg had gone cold.

'I'll go and give Johnny a shout.' Colin went out into the hall.

'And tell him to have a shower,' Nina called after him. 'Eat up, Holly!' she urged her. 'You want to have some energy for the country.'

What would she be expected to do there? Holly wondered. She suspected she was not going to like the place. Her class had gone to an outdoor centre for a week last summer but her mum wouldn't let her go. She'd said she couldn't afford it.

When Holly had finished eating, Nina suggested she go upstairs and pack.

'I want us to be out of here as soon as possible! Evangeline might take it into her head to bring her American friend round after all.'

'I wouldn't put it past her,' said Colin.

'Neither would I!'

Holly raced up the stairs and put her few bits and pieces back in her bag. She didn't have much with her, just the trousers and top she was wearing, a couple of other tops and clean pants and socks. Her mum had said not to take too much since her dad would buy her new clothes.

Nina put her head round the door. 'How're you getting on?'

'OK.'

'Are those the only shoes you've got with you?' She examined Holly's black patents with the silver buckles. 'They won't be any good in the country. The soles are way too thin.'

'My dad was going to buy me some new clothes. He always does.'

'That's good.' Nina was still pursing her lips as she surveyed Holly's clothing. Her pale lilac trousers were made of thin cotton and her outdoor jacket was not very thick. Nor was it lined.

'My mum didn't know I'd be going to the country.'

'Of course she didn't. Don't worry about it.'

The Nightingales were always telling her not to worry but she couldn't help it.

'We'll go into Pitlochry on the way and buy you some warmer clothing.'

Holly tried to speak but Nina wouldn't listen.

'You can't go into the country in those thin clothes, love. You'd freeze to death. I'd better go and chivvy Johnny now or we won't get away till lunchtime.'

After Holly had zipped up her bag she ventured out on to the landing. She was dreading this trip. Would she have to sit in the back seat of the car with Johnny?

'You'll find out soon enough,' said Sylvie.

The kitchen door must have been open for the raised voices of Johnny and his mother could be clearly heard.

'Why should *she* come with us to the cottage when Tim can't?'

'Her name is *Holly* and not *she*. Holly is coming with us and I don't want to hear another word about it. Do you imagine we would leave her here in the house on her own?'

'Why can't Tim come as well?'

'Two boys would be too much for Holly to cope with. She's having to adjust to enough things without that.'

'So it's because of *her* I can't have Tim?'

'Look, I'm not discussing it any further. You should have asked me before you asked Tim anyway.'

'In that case I won't go to the cottage either. I'll go and stay at Tim's. His mum says I'm welcome any time.'

'You're coming with us.' Colin's voice joined in now. 'And don't shout at your mother. Or me, either.'

'This is nuts!' Johnny didn't seem to be keeping his voice down too much. 'Because of that stupid girl whose mother dumped her on you I can't even have *my* best friend with me on holiday. It's not fair!'

Sylvie could see his point of view. So, unfortunately, could Holly, who was feeling unhappy again. Her mood kept swinging this way and that. This whole row was her fault. Perhaps they should just do a runner and then Johnny could have Tim to stay.

'Don't be daft,' scolded Sylvie. 'They'd have the police after you right away. They've promised your dad they'll look after you.'

'Well, it isn't fair, is it?' Johnny wasn't giving up. 'And don't tell me life's not fair! You've told me that a hundred times over.'

Colin told him to go upstairs and pack his bag. He came sloping out of the kitchen with his head down. Holly scuttled back into her room and shut the door before he caught sight of her.

She wished his mother had let him go to his pal's. It would have made her life easier. Sylvie said she would just have to ignore him, but that might be difficult in the country. It would be easier in town for he seemed to spend a lot of time having sleepovers at other boys' houses. Holly herself had never had a sleepover but Sylvie had, several times, and knew all about them. It seemed that nobody did much sleeping and you might have to share a bed with two or three girls. Once Sylvie had had to sleep right on the edge and had fallen out in the middle of the night and sprained her wrist.

Nina's head reappeared round the door. 'Ready, Holly?'

Johnny had the front seat of the car beside his father, Nina climbed into the back with Holly. Johnny sat staring straight ahead, not speaking.

'Still in the huff, obviously,' commented Sylvie.

As they were backing out of the drive another car came sweeping past, almost clipping their rear-end, which caused Colin to swerve and swear. It was a big square vehicle.

The car had screeched to a halt a few metres further along.

'I can't believe it,' cried Nina. 'It's Evangeline and she's got a passenger!'

'And a dog,' added Johnny, finding his voice.

The animal was looking out of the back window of the car. Holly leaned forward to look. It was a big dog with a large head and Holly was glad it was safely inside another car. A man along their street had a nasty dog that had chased her one day and nearly nipped her ankles. Her mum had complained to the owner, who'd told her to drop dead, or something like that.

'Don't stop!' cried Nina.

Colin pulled briskly away from the kerb.

Nina didn't wave or look round. 'It takes a lot to put her off.'

'You've got some funny friends,' said Johnny.

His mother didn't reply to that.

They settled into their journey. Johnny and his dad talked about rugby. The back-seat passengers didn't talk as much but every now and then Nina would point something out, to keep Holly informed of their whereabouts. It was a bit like having a geography lesson but Holly didn't mind. She liked being told things.

'We're going over the Forth Road Bridge now.' They were crossing a very wide stretch of water. 'Have you ever been on it before?'

Holly had not.

'And that's the rail bridge over there. It's very famous.'

Holly turned her head to look. 'We took a train over there once, my dad and me,' she said excitedly. 'He rented a cottage in a wee place at the sea called Aberdour. We had a great time. He's good fun, my dad.'

'You must have enjoyed that.'

'My mum can be fun too,' Holly added quickly. When Lenny was out of the way they often had a good laugh together.

'I'm sure she can.' They had left the bridge behind. 'We're on the A9 now and heading north.'

After they'd been on the road for over an hour Nina announced that they were about to turn off to Pitlochry. 'We're in Perthshire now.'

Pitlochry! Wasn't that the place where Nina had said she'd buy her some clothes?

'You don't have to buy me anything,' said Holly in a low voice so that Johnny wouldn't hear.

'We've already discussed that, dear.'

When Nina made up her mind she didn't change it, said Sylvie. Best just to go along with it.

Colin managed to find a parking space in the main street. They split up and arranged to meet later. Colin set off down the street with Johnny, and Holly followed Nina.

The town was busy with tourists. Most were dawdling along, eating ice creams or looking into shop windows. Nina led the way into a large store that seemed to sell lots of outdoor country clothes like anoraks and fleeces. It wasn't the kind of shop Holly's mum would fancy at all.

'Now I think you could do with a fleece to start with.' Nina trawled along a rail and took one or two down. She held them out. 'What colour would you like? Red, blue, black, navy?'

Holly chose red. She had to try it on so that Nina could make sure it fitted.

'It's a little on the big side but you'll grow into it. They're two for the price of one so you may as well have the second one. How about blue? It's a nice deep blue. Cornflower blue. It would be a perfect match for your eyes.'

Holly blushed. No one had ever mentioned her eyes before.

By the time they left the shop they had two bulging bags filled with one red fleece, and one blue, two sweatshirts, one royal blue, one primrose yellow, a pair of jeans, trainers (white with red flashes) and three pairs of warm socks of various colours.

'That's an awful lot,' protested Holly.

'None of it was expensive. This is a cheap store and nearly everything was on offer.'

'My dad will –'

'Now we've been through all that, Holly.'

Nina was not in a mood to be argued with today. That Evangeline woman had well and truly got her dander up. So had Johnny.

Yes, *Johnny*. Holly had managed to forget him whilst they were shopping.

He stared at the huge bags.

'Have you bought her all *that*?' he asked.

Nina ignored his question and carried on towards the car.

'I bet you didn't get me anything?' grumped Johnny when he'd caught her up.

'You have more than enough clothes as it is.'

'You certainly do,' agreed his father.

'Johnny's going to hate you,' Sylvie said to Holly.

'He already does,' said Holly.

Twelve

The Nightingales' cottage sat in the lee of the Cairngorm mountains in Inverness-shire. It was a lot colder up there than in Edinburgh at that time of year, as Holly was quick to find out. She'd shivered in her thin shoes and jacket when they'd got out of the car and was now in her room changing into something warmer. Johnny had whizzed off up the glen on his bike straightaway. A good idea, his father had said. It would work off some of his aggro.

Once dressed, Holly decided she'd better go through to the sitting room. She hesitated outside the door, hearing voices. They were talking about Johnny.

'His nose has been put out of joint,' his father was saying.

'That's because of you,' said Sylvie.

Holly hardly needed Sylvie to point that out.

'It has all been sprung on him without warning,' said Nina.

'Us too.'

'Yes, but he's only thirteen. We need to give him some attention too.'

'I know. I'll take him off for the day tomorrow. We might even be able to get a bit of skiing in. There's still some snow on the tops.'

Holly was thankful she wouldn't be expected to go skiing with them.

'You'd better go in,' advised Sylvie. 'You can't stand there all day.'

Holly opened the door.

'Come on in!' cried Colin. 'Come and sit by the fire.'

A log fire was crackling in the grate. Holly had never seen a fire like that before. People didn't seem to have them in the town. She and her mum had electric radiators.

She felt awkward standing there in the stiff new jeans and primrose yellow sweatshirt. They didn't feel like they belonged to her.

'You look lovely in that shade of yellow,' said Nina.

Holly tugged the sweatshirt around her waist. 'It's sort of, well, kind of big. And the jeans.' She peered down at them.

'No, they're not. They're clothes for the country. You wouldn't want to wear them skintight. You need to be able to move around freely. You'll feel more comfortable, believe me!'

Holly went up to the fire and crouched in front of the flames.

'Nice smell, isn't it?' said Colin.

Holly nodded.

He announced that he was going out to chop some fresh logs. He left Holly with Nina.

'Would you like to go for a walk in the wood?' asked Nina. 'It'd be a pity not to, it's such a lovely day.'

Sun was streaming in through the big, floor-length

window. From there they had a wide view up the glen into the hills. Sheep were grazing in the next field. It was very peaceful. Nina sighed and said it was great to get away from the noise and bustle of the city. Holly was not so sure.

'So, shall we go for a walk?' Nina got up. 'Just a short one. We could both do with some exercise and fresh air. Blow the cobwebs away! Put a fleece on, you'll probably need it.'

'I feel all bundled up,' said Holly, when she'd got the fleece on and Nina had helped to sort out the zip, which she'd managed to get stuck at the bottom.

'It'll keep the wind out.'

Holly stuck her hands deep into the pockets and followed Nina out, head down. They passed Colin on their way up the garden. He seemed to be enjoying chopping logs.

'Great exercise!' he declared. 'We'll bake some spuds in the fire tonight, Holly.'

'You're going to put them right inside the fire?' Holly was shocked.

'I certainly am!' Colin laughed at her expression.

Everybody knows that baked potatoes are cooked in a microwave, thought Holly.

They left him to get on with his log-chopping and crossed the lane over to a wood. Holly stepped uncertainly on to the path that snaked its way between the dark green trees.

'They're evergreens,' said Nina. 'Firs and pines.'

Holly hesitated. She looked down at her brand-new

trainers. Those were the things she liked most of all the clothes that Nina had bought her.

'I don't want to get my new trainers dirty.'

'The path's not muddy. It's quite dry, in fact. It feels nice and soft, that's from the fallen pine needles.'

It was quiet in the wood, apart from the soft tread of their feet and a bird that was calling from a treetop nearby. Holly kept glancing around as if she wasn't sure what to expect.

Suddenly an animal sprang from a group of trees on their left and leapt across the path to vanish into the wood on the other side. Holly gulped back a scream.

'What was it?'

'A deer. A roe deer. We've got a lot of them round here.'

'What a fright it gave me!'

'They wouldn't hurt you.'

'Are you sure?'

'They're nervous of you. That's why they run away.'

'Are there any other animals going about?'

'Plenty! Rabbits, hares, field mice –'

'I hate mice. We had one in the kitchen. It ate the fur in my mum's new boots and walked over the fat in the frying pan. You could see the marks of its feet.'

'That wasn't so good.'

'Lenny set a trap for it at night with a lump of cheese. It looked horrible in the morning all squashed up.'

'Well, you don't need to worry about that here. The field mice stay in the fields, in summertime anyway.'

But it wasn't summer yet, thought Holly. 'They wouldn't come into my bedroom? Or climb up my bed?'

'Absolutely not.'

Holly was not totally convinced.

'We have squirrels too.' She could see that Nina was changing the topic. 'Red squirrels. There's one that comes into the gardens and eats the nuts from our bird feeder.'

'You don't have no wolves but?'

'No, no wolves.'

Sylvie said, 'What about spiders?' They gave Holly the creeps. She asked Nina.

'You might see the odd one. But they don't come out in hundreds!'

'Just as well,' commented Sylvie.

'And if you see one just yell,' Nina went on, 'and Colin will come and remove it. I have to confess I'm not fond of spiders myself. Yet I know they're harmless.'

She glanced up. The sky had suddenly clouded over, blocking out the sun, and the wood had darkened. They had gone only a few more steps before they felt the first drops of rain on their faces.

Nina seemed reluctant to turn back but she thought that perhaps they'd better. Holly was relieved. Within seconds the drops had developed into a thorough downpour and they had to run for the house.

'My new fleece is all wet,' wailed Holly. She was surprised at how upset she was about it.

'It'll dry. Here, hang it with my fleece over.'

'And my trainers have got some dirt on them.'

'They'll clean. Go and sit by the fire and get warm.'

'Yes, come on in, Holly,' called Colin. 'I've got some really good flames going.'

Holly crouched as close as she could to the roaring fire, warming her hands. She looked deep into the vivid orange flames. You could almost see pictures in there. She pointed out a man's face to Sylvie. And didn't that look like a witch's hat? Colin warned her to move back a bit but she didn't do it quickly enough and in the next instant a spark had flown out and struck her right in the chest, in the middle of her primrose yellow sweatshirt. Holly yelled and fell backwards.

Colin grabbed her and crushed out the flame with his hand. Her sweatshirt now had a big ugly brown scorch mark which looked as if it might turn into a hole and Colin had rushed to the sink to hold his hand under cold water. It was all too much.

Holly burst into tears.

Holly hardly ever cried. She hadn't cried when she'd been told that her mum had gone off with Lenny the Louse on holiday. She hadn't cried when she'd found that her dad wasn't at home in his flat. She'd managed not to cry when she discovered he wasn't coming back for two whole weeks. But she was crying now because her lovely new yellow top was ruined! And that nasty lump of a boy Johnny had just come in and was standing in the middle of the room dripping wet and smirking.

Nina came and put her arms round her. 'It's all right, love. You're not hurt, are you?'

'But Colin!' cried Holly. 'He's burnt his hand 'cos of me.' There seemed to be no end to the troubles she could cause.

'No, he hasn't, not badly, have you, Colin?'

He squatted down beside them and showed her the palm of his hand. 'See, it's just a bit pink. I got it under cold water straightaway and that took the heat out of it. That's what I always do when I burn myself.'

'And my top.' Holly couldn't take her eyes off the burn. She really had liked the primrose colour.

'We'll get you a new one,' said Nina.

'Of course you will,' murmured Johnny, though loud enough for everyone to hear.

His mother turned and frowned at him but he didn't seem bothered. He was shaking his head and scattering raindrops everywhere.

'Look through him!' said Sylvie. 'Pretend he doesn't exist! That's the way to cope with him.'

Holly couldn't see how she could ignore him with all of them together in this one room. It was a very big room, she couldn't deny that, with windows on all four sides, but there was no separate kitchen – it was in an alcove – and there was no other sitting room. There was nowhere else to go. And Nina and Colin didn't have the studies that they had in Edinburgh. Nina had explained to Holly that this was the place she escaped to for peace and quiet. As well as to write, of course. She'd said she was in the middle of a book and was dying to get on with it. Holly couldn't see how she'd manage to do that, not on this holiday.

Nina was talking to her. 'Go and take the sweatshirt off, Holly. I'll bin it. Put on your other one.'

'I feel awful.'

'Don't! Accidents happen. And this one is not the biggest disaster in the world.'

Perhaps not, thought Holly, but she still felt upset. She passed Johnny without looking sideways at him and went through to her bedroom to change her sweatshirt. This room was small with a window at one end that looked deep into the branches of a lilac tree. Nina had told her it was a lilac and that the buds were waiting to open, as long as a late frost didn't get them first, which it often did. Holly could believe that. The window was awash with rain. Behind it the tree and the rest of the garden were a green blur. Nina had switched on the central heating but it was the kind that came on overnight so the house wouldn't warm up properly until morning. Sometimes Holly and her mum didn't put their electric radiator on at all as the woman below, who was elderly, kept her flat like a furnace and they got the benefit from the heat upstairs. It saved putting too much money in the electricity meter. Sometimes her mum didn't have enough anyway.

Thinking about her mum brought a lump to Holly's throat. Was she wearing her new turquoise and pink bikini and lying on a beach in the sunshine? Her mum loved the sun. She said she felt a different person. One night Lenny had suggested they move to Spain to live. Relocate. The way people did in those television programmes. Buy an old ruin for hardly any money and do it up. They'd got all excited about it. Lenny had said there was no reason why they shouldn't go for it. Sharon could get a job in a club or a bar and he could do odd jobs. He'd heard there was plenty of that kind of work out there, doing up other people's ruins. He was good at making and mending things. Even Holly acknowledged that. He'd fixed their washing machine and put up shelves in the kitchen.

Holly was alarmed now. They hadn't gone and done it, had they? Relocated? Without telling her? They wouldn't, would they, and leave her behind?

Thirteen

'You're letting your imagination carry you away again,' said Sylvie.

'They were really keen to go though, to Spain.'

'Maybe they were,' Lenny was always full of big plans, 'but then your mum reminded him that they'd no money. Remember?'

Holly remembered. Sharon had sighed and said to Lenny, 'You'd need some money, wouldn't you, to relocate? To get started. To buy the ruin.'

Lenny suggested they put extra money on the lottery for a week or two. Well, you never knew, did you? You might get lucky. Some people must. He knew somebody whose cousin had won three million. But you couldn't believe everything Lenny told you.

They had even talked of Holly going to school in Spain and how she'd learn to speak Spanish. She'd liked the idea of that. One of Nina's books about Sylvie had been set in Spain. Sylvie had liked it, out there, in Spain. She'd stayed in a pretty white village in the hills.

'So you see,' Sylvie went on now, 'they *did* intend to take you with them. Otherwise they wouldn't have said that, would they? About you learning Spanish.'

Still, Holly felt uneasy. She didn't trust Lenny. He took money from her mum at times. He'd come in saying he was skint, could she lend him a couple of tenners? He didn't ever pay it back even though he always promised he would. Sylvie said Holly's mum was a soft touch. She never seemed to learn.

Holly sat on the edge of the bed in her clean new royal blue sweatshirt. She was going to stay well away from the wood fire in this top! The fire might smell lovely but it was dangerous too, as she'd discovered.

She decided to take out her notebook. She hadn't had much time to write in it since she'd come to stay with the Nightingales. It wasn't a diary about herself so much as notes about other people. She wrote about the snooty Smithereens and pain-in-the-neck Evangeline. Better not write anything about Johnny, advised Sylvie. 'In case he finds it!'

After a few minutes Holly's fingers were beginning to turn blue. Sylvie thought they should go back to the nice warm sitting room.

'Don't freeze to death because of that idiot! Nina and Colin won't let him off if he's rude to you. They'll stick up for you.'

Holly stayed where she was. Every time Johnny's mum and dad told him off he'd hate her even more.

'You can't sit in here all week.'

'I might have to.'

'Don't talk daft! And you needn't think about trying to do a runner, not from a place like this.'

Holly herself knew that was not on. Doing a runner was difficult enough in the city but at least it had streets and alleyways and parks and corners where you could hide. Where could you go here? Colin had told her that if you headed up the glen you'd end up deep inside the high mountains, miles and miles from any habitation. You'd find yourself in the wilderness. Where you could get lost and wander for days and days and never be found and there could be all sorts of creatures lurking about. Holly wasn't sure she believed Nina about the wolves. This would be a perfect place for wolves. Her teacher had told the class that some people wanted to re-introduce them to Scotland. They used to live here, a long time ago. Holly was glad she wasn't alive then.

'There's no way out,' said Sylvie. 'You've got to make the best of it. And him.'

The door opened and Nina poked her head in. 'There you are! I'm just starting to get the supper ready. Maybe you'd like to give me a hand, set the table, perhaps? And, Holly, don't let Johnny bother you. He's got to adjust to things too.'

There was no sign of him in the sitting room. He must have gone to his room. It was still raining. Holly set the table and folded the paper serviettes into shapes like little boats. Her mum had once worked once as a waitress in a posh restaurant and been taught to do that. She used to get some nice food to bring home afterwards and Holly had wished she'd kept her job there. But the club paid better.

'I've made a chicken casserole.' Nina carried it over to the table. 'I hope you like chicken?'

Holly did.

Nina admired the napkins and then asked Colin to give Johnny a shout to tell him supper was ready.

He came slouching in and the first things that caught his eye were the perky little red boats. He picked his up and shook it out.

'I thought you hated serviettes twisted into fancy shapes, Mum? You said they were pretentious.'

Nina looked levelly at him. 'I think they look very attractive.'

'He knows full well you must have done them,' said Sylvie.

They sat down to eat and Colin talked about a pheasant family that had lived in their garden the year before. At one point there had been seven young, though by the time the summer ended they had been reduced to three. He thought a fox must have got them. Were there foxes in the garden? Holly wanted to ask, but she didn't for she knew Johnny would sneer at her.

'The foxes only come out at night,' said Nina, as if she could read Holly's thoughts.

After the meal Colin washed up and Holly dried. She offered to do it. She usually did the dishes at home.

'Your turn tomorrow, Johnny,' said Colin.

Johnny made a face. 'Why don't we get a dishwasher here? Like we have at home.'

'We manage fine without one. And it saves electricity.'

They had no television either. Holly wondered what they were going to do all evening. She had almost finished her book.

They all settled down around the fire to read, even

Johnny. He seemed to be deep into his book and every now and then he laughed out loud, but he didn't tell them what the joke was. Holly reached the end of her book far too quickly. Sylvie pointed out that she could always start at the beginning again. She often did.

'Finished your book?' asked Nina. 'Have you got anything else to read? No? Dash it, I meant to bring some for you but forgot with everything else going on.'

'Oh yes, Evangeline!' Colin nodded his head. 'That was what was going on. I expect she's still fuming. You've never given her our phone number here, have you?'

'Certainly not! I'm careful about who I give it to.'

'Just as well.'

'I'll buy you a couple of books tomorrow in the shop in Aviemore, Holly,' said Nina. 'I've got to go in anyway. I promised I'd sign some of my books for them.'

Colin was looking out of the window. 'I believe the rain has stopped. Why don't we go for a walk up the glen before the light goes?'

Another walk!

'On the road this time, Holly,' said Nina. 'We don't go into the wood when it's getting dark. Too easy to get lost. Away and put your fleece on.'

'You coming, Johnny?' asked his father.

Johnny chose to go on his bike.

'Not too far now,' cautioned his mother. 'It'll be dark in half an hour.'

Colin put two more big logs on the fire and arranged the fireguard carefully around it.

By the time the rest of them were ready Johnny had

taken off and was out of sight. Holly, wearing her dry blue fleece, walked between Nina and Colin. Nina told her to inhale and take a breath of air.

'Doesn't it smell fresh and sweet?'

'Good for the lungs,' added Colin.

Holly supposed he would think of that, with him being a doctor. She did as she had been told, and nodded though she was not sure it was any different to the air in Glasgow.

'There must be a difference,' insisted Sylvie. 'Without all the nasty traffic fumes you get in town.'

No vehicle passed them. The clouds had parted to let in a little of the late evening sun and the hillside shone pink in the reflected light. A large dark bird passed low overheard. The burn, as they crossed the bridge that straddled it, made a soft rushing sound. The rest of the glen was hushed. Even the sheep seemed to have gone to sleep. They walked without talking and after about fifteen minutes turned and retraced their steps.

The sun had dropped below the horizon, the hill was colourless now. The fir trees at the other side of the field were just black shapes. There was no moon. And no streetlights. Holly shivered. The air might not be as clean in Glasgow but at least the streets were lit and you could see where you were going.

'Time Johnny was coming back.' Nina peered back along the shadowy road.

'Expect he'll be home soon.' His father seemed less worried. 'There's no traffic about.'

'Unless he's gone off-road.'

'Shouldn't think he'd be that stupid.'

They went into the warm room.

Johnny didn't came back for another three-quarters of an hour. By that time it was completely dark and both his parents were getting anxious. Holly heard Nina say quietly to Colin that she suspected he was doing it deliberately, to worry them and get attention and Colin agreed.

'He'll be all right, though. He's got working lights on the bike.'

When Johnny did come in there was a big row. Holly escaped to her bedroom. She was dead tired anyway, with all that walking and fresh air. When Johnny went into his room, which was next door to hers, he slammed the door. She felt the vibration through the wall.

Fourteen

Holly was wakened early by a strange noise outside. She tugged the curtain aside to see a big bird with reddish-brown feathers and a green chest strutting up the garden as if he owned the place. It must be one of the pheasants Colin had been talking about the night before. He was making quite a noise. The small birds were already chirping up in the trees, even though it was barely light.

Holly slipped back into sleep and when she awoke again she was pleased to see that the sun was shining. The only clouds in sight were a few little white puffy ones. Johnny would be able to go out on his bike. If it were raining they'd all be stuck inside the house.

Holly joined Nina and Colin for breakfast. This was the nicest part of the day, with just the three of them eating together. She wished it could stay that way. If only Johnny could have been left behind in Edinburgh!

'Not very nice of you thinking that,' chided Sylvie. 'After all, it is *his* house!'

'Johnny does seem to need an awful lot of sleep these days,' commented Nina.

'Nothing to worry about,' said his father. 'He's active enough the rest of the time.'

'I think he's been having too many sleepovers recently.'

Colin decided to do a few chores to outside. Nina

spent the time weeding her flower border while Holly hung around watching. She felt a bit of a spare part at first, but when she offered to help, Nina gave her a hoe and showed her how to use it. After a while, Nina looked at her watch. 'We really should be off to Aviemore,' she called to Colin. 'But Johnny's still sleeping. Or at least, he hasn't got out of his bed.'

'Leave him,' said his father. 'I don't suppose he'd want to come with us anyway. He hates shopping.'

Nina left a note for him on the table.

Twenty minutes later they were in the resort village of Aviemore. Colin parked and they did some shopping for food first of all, then he went to the ironmonger's while Nina and Holly made for the bookshop.

Nina introduced Holly to the manager, who asked Holly if she liked books.

'Oh, I do! Especially Nina Nightingale books.'

'You've got a fan there, Nina!'

'Seems I do. There's nothing nicer than meeting your readers – and this one seems to know more about my books than I do.'

Nina and the manager exchanged smiles.

'Why don't you have a look around the shelves and see if there's something you like. And don't pick mine! You can read those for free when we get back to Edinburgh!'

The manager brought out a pile of Nina's books for her to sign and Holly went up to the back of the shop. After a good browse around the shelves she chose *Anne of Green Gables* and *Anne of the Island*. She'd borrowed them both from her local library but she wanted copies of her own to keep. She took out her purse and counted out the money.

When she took them to the till she laid the money on the counter.

'I was going to pay for them,' protested Nina.

'I've got my own pocket money,' said Holly determinedly.

For a moment it looked as if Nina might argue, then she said, 'OK then, that's fine.'

Colin caught up with them outside the shop.

'We've got to replace Holly's sweatshirt,' Nina reminded him.

'We don't need to,' put in Holly. 'I'm not going to burn this one. I'm never going to go close to the fire again.'

'But if it rains you might get it wet. You really do need another to change into.'

'Only if you let me pay.'

'Don't give in,' urged Sylvie.

Holly did not intend to.

Nina sighed. 'You don't want to spend your pocket money on clothes.'

'Why not?'

'I'd rather you kept it for special things. Like books. Chocolate. Or ice cream.'

'My dad will give me more money when he comes.'

'Well, let's see how much you've got then, Holly.' Nina gave in with a smile.

They went to a store belonging to the same chain as the one in Pitlochry and found a primrose yellow sweatshirt, the twin of the one that had been scorched. Holly showed

Nina that she had enough money to pay for it, and a little to spare. Enough for an ice cream anyway, if she wanted one. And since the sweatshirts were on sale two for one, Nina said it would be foolish not to take a second one so Holly chose a green top as well.

Then she paid.

'That's *three* I'll have altogether!'

'They'll all come in useful,' said Nina.

Colin announced that he was hungry and proposed they went for a bite of lunch. 'Just a bowl of soup and a panini, something simple like that. Suit you OK, Holly?'

'Yes, thank you.'

'It's good you've stopped saying "Uh-huh",' approved Sylvie. 'Well, more or less.'

They walked up the street to a café. Holly walked between Nina and Colin, swinging her sweatshirt bag in one hand and the bookshop bag in the other. She had to let Colin pay for the lunch. He told her straightaway that it was not up for discussion.

'I invited you.'

The café was one floor up so they had a wide view of the Cairngorm mountains. There was snow on the tops. They looked pretty, thought Holly, as long as she didn't have to go up there. Colin did, with Johnny, when they went skiing.

'I hope that boy will be up by now,' said Nina as they returned to the car after lunch and headed homeward.

'He won't be sleeping all this time,' said Colin. 'Surely not!'

'Surely nothing!' Nina replied. 'He can sleep for hours.'

But Johnny was up. His bed was empty and he'd had breakfast, which his mother could tell from the dirty dishes left in the sink. And his bike was gone from the shed.

'He must have gone for a run,' said Colin.

'He could have left a note,' complained Nina. 'To say where he was going.'

'He wouldn't think to.'

'I left him one!'

'That's different. You're his mother.'

Colin had decided to do a barbecue for supper so that Nina wouldn't have to think about cooking.

'Why don't you take some time on your book? You've not had much chance to get on with it recently.'

They looked at Holly.

'I can read,' she said quickly.

'Maybe not all afternoon,' said Nina. 'Do you like doing jigsaws?'

'Don't know.' Suddenly Holly felt a little nervous.

'You'll have done some, I'm sure?'

'Might have when I was at nursery.'

Nina pulled out a stack of jigsaws. There were boxes and boxes of them. Some had 1,000 pieces but she found one with only 500, which had a picture of a Scottish castle on the lid. Nina tumbled the pieces out on to the table.

'This is one of my favourites,' she said, 'I'll help you get started.'

She spent half an hour with Holly and then left her

to get on with the rest of it while she went round to her desk, which was tucked away out of sight behind the free-standing stone fireplace. It was out of sight, but not, of course, sound.

A few minutes later the phone rang. For a moment, Holly wondered about answering it, so that Nina wouldn't be disturbed, but it wasn't her house, and she didn't know what she would say. Colin must be outside.

Nina didn't look pleased before she lifted the receiver but she was even less so once she discovered who was at the other end. '*Evangeline!*' she gasped, as if she couldn't believe her ears. 'How did you get our number?' There was a pause. 'You rang Claire Edwards? But you've never met her, have you?' Nina raised her eyebrows. 'You found her number in the book?'

Evangeline rambled on at the other end of the line, silencing Nina for a while. Eventually she broke in. 'A piece of luck? What are you talking about? What about your American friends – ?' She was cut off again. She frowned. 'They're setting off on a tour of the Highlands? Now listen, Evangeline, *please*,' Nina was almost shouting, which Holly realized was the only way to get her message across. 'I'm very sorry but we don't receive visitors here. This is our secret bolt hole.'

Another volley from Evangeline.

'I'm sorry if I sound inhospitable,' Nina continued. 'No, not *even* for an hour. I am extremely busy. I'm in the middle of a book and I must go. Goodbye!' She dumped down the receiver.

'She's not coming, is she?' asked Holly. 'She sounds 'orrible.'

'Horrible,' murmured Sylvie, stressing the 'H'.

'Certainly not! Coming here?! Nor are her American friends. And she *can* be horrible at times.'

Quite often, thought Holly.

Nina went over to the sink, ran the cold tap and took a long drink of water. Then she returned to her desk. No sooner than she had done so than the phone rang.

'Not again!' she cried.

She came striding round to answer it. Holly could see she was at the end of her tether.

'She must be,' said Sylvie. 'Not being able to get on with her book.'

'Evangeline,' Nina started and then she changed her voice. 'Oh, it's you, Claire!' She listened. 'It's all right, don't apologize! I know what Evangeline is like. A bulldozer. She won't give way. I'm sure she had a good story. *What*? She said an American writer had arranged to see me to fix up a book deal but had lost my address? The nerve of her!'

'What a liar!' thought Holly.

'You didn't give it to her though, did you?' Nina asked anxiously. 'Only the phone number? Thank goodness for that at least!'

She ended up having a half-hour chat with Claire about this and that.

'She'll never get her book written at this rate,' commented Sylvie.

Holly wasn't making much progress with her

jigsaw either. She was too busy listening to Nina's conversations.

On the way back to her desk, Nina stopped beside Holly to see how she was getting on and helped her find two or three pieces.

'If the phone rings again do you think you could answer it, Holly?'

'Of course.'

'And tell whoever it is that I am unavailable. I'd love to get the damned thing taken out but of course I can't. In case of an emergency and Colin was needed. The mobile phone signal isn't very strong up here.'

For at least ten minutes there was peace and quiet. Until the phone rang again.

Holly jumped up quickly and lifted the receiver.

'Nina, they want to know if you'd like double glazing for your windows?'

'Tell them no!'

'No, thank you,' said Holly. 'She doesn't.'

'Thanks, love,' said Nina.

'I like answering the phone.'

'Good. You can do it any time you like.'

'Do you mean it?'

'Absolutely. You're in charge of it from now on. It's the bane of my life. I can't remember where I am in this book and what I'd been planning to do with the characters next. Dump them in the loch perhaps?'

'Not Sylvie!'

'It's all right. Sylvie can swim anyway.'

'Course I can.' Sylvie was scornful.

Colin appeared at the window. 'Cup of tea?' he mouthed, bringing an imaginary cup to his mouth.

'I think Colin's asking if you want a cup of tea,' said Holly.

'Oh, I suppose I might as well.' Nina appeared from around the corner again. 'I'm not achieving anything else at the moment.'

'I'll make it.' Holly went and put the kettle on.

She poured the tea when it was ready and Colin opened a packet of chocolate ginger biscuits.

'Nina's favourites,' he told Holly.

Holly liked them too. They sat round the fire drinking tea and eating biscuits. It wasn't so bad after all, a cottage in the country. Colin said that a wind had sprung up outside. Inside, the room felt warm and cosy.

'Get much done?' Colin asked Nina.

'You must be joking!' She told him about all the phone calls.

'Evangeline should be locked up,' he declared.

'I don't think that American woman – Mariposa was it? – will manage to find us.'

'Fortunately there are a lot of glens in the Highlands.'

'And I have never told Evangeline the name of ours.' Nina looked at her watch. She'd done that once or twice, Holly had noticed. 'Johnny's been gone a long time, don't you think? It's half-past six.'

'He might have called in at Jamie's.' Jamie was a boy of about Johnny's age who lived up at the head of the glen, Colin explained to Holly.

'I'll give his mother a ring,' said Nina.

But Jamie's mother hadn't seen Johnny that day.

'If he does turn up would you tell him to come home straightaway?' asked Nina. 'Thanks.'

She stood beside the telephone, frowning.

'Would he have his mobile on him?' wondered Colin.

'He should do. I always tell him to take it when he goes off on his own.'

'I'll go and check his room.'

Colin came back carrying the phone in his hand. 'It was lying on his bed.'

'I'm a bit worried,' announced Nina, though that was obvious.

'I'm sure nothing will have happened to him. He can look after himself. But I'll take a run up to the head of the glen, if you like, and see if there's any sign of him or his bike.'

'Yes, do that.'

After he'd gone Holly asked Nina, 'Do you think Johnny might have got lost?'

'He shouldn't do. He knows the area like the back of his hand.'

Colin was away for well over half an hour. Nina couldn't sit still. She moved about the room, looking out of each of the four windows in turn. The branches of the lilac tree were tossing in the wind, which had strengthened considerably. And the sky had darkened.

'It's going to rain,' commented Nina.

Holly washed up. As she was tidying away the tea things Colin came back in. He, too, now looked concerned.

'I found his bike. It was lying at the side of the road.'

'Where?' asked Nina.

'Near the path where you cut across to go up on to the ridge.'

'He knows he's not allowed to go up on to the ridge by himself.'

'Well, yes, he does. But I have a feeling that might be where he has gone.' Colin grabbed the car keys from the dresser.

Fifteen

They drove up the glen to the place where Colin had seen Johnny's bike. It was still lying there in the long grass at the side of the road.

'I left it in case he'd come back for it.'

Holly was beginning to feel worried herself. Until now she'd just felt glad Johnny was out of the way. She might not like him all that much but she wouldn't want anything bad to happen to him.

Colin had brought his binoculars along. He had them trained on the ridge and the slopes leading up to it.

'Can you see anything?' asked Nina.

'The light's too poor.'

'What are we going to do?'

'It's difficult to know whether to call out the Mountain Rescue or not.' Colin pursed his lips. 'We don't know whether Johnny has actually gone up there, or not. I'd hate to call them out on a false alarm.'

'The trouble is,' said Sylvie to Holly 'he might be hiding in the trees further up the road, just to worry them.'

'I'd hate *not* to call them out when he might be lying up there injured or lost,' said Nina. Holly noticed a sharpness in her tone.

'This is what is known as a dilemma,' said Sylvie. She had been involved in a number of those herself, of course. Put there by Nina. But this was none of Nina's doing.

'I'm going to walk up the track to the foot of the hill,' said Colin. 'I've brought a whistle.'

'Don't go any further,' urged Nina. 'You might get lost too.'

'Don't worry. You and Holly wait in the car.'

The wait seemed interminable. Rain started running down the car windows blurring the outside world. Neither Nina nor Holly spoke.

When Colin returned he was soaked. He got into the car shaking his head and scattering raindrops.

'It's hopeless. The weather is really closing in now. We'll have to go home and phone the police. I can't get a signal here.

'It's the mountains that get in the way,' Nina explained to Holly.

Once back in the house Colin went straight to the phone without even taking off his wet jacket. He explained the situation, apologizing, saying he hoped he wouldn't be bringing them out on a fool's errand. 'But we are very worried,' he added.

They sat waiting until help arrived in the form of one police car and four Land Rovers. As Colin explained, the people who made up the rescue team were volunteers and had other jobs. Nor did they necessarily live nearby. They'd have come from glens and villages all over Speyside.

Colin, with Nina and Holly in the back seat, drove up the glen again to show the men where Johnny's bike lay abandoned. It was completely dark now.

Four men emerged from each Land Rover, wearing climbing boots and heavy anoraks and armed with ropes, axes, torches and whistles. They were also carrying First Aid kits and parachute flares that they could let off to light up the hillside. Two collie dogs accompanied them and the police had brought an Alsatian. The dogs were all on leads, Holly was glad to see.

The road, which was usually quiet but for the passing of an occasional car and the bleat of sheep, was suddenly full of people and dogs and noise. Holly stepped out of the way on to the grass verge.

'Sorry to bring you all out,' said Colin, shouting into the wind. 'We can't be one hundred per cent certain –'

'Don't worry.' The leader of the group cut him off. 'Better to be safe than sorry. Thirteen, did you say he was? Not that experienced on the hills, then?'

'He's been out with me quite often so he's not stupid. But he's never gone off on his own like this.'

The man didn't ask anything more. Just as well, Sylvie remarked to Holly, since Johnny's mum and dad wouldn't have wanted to tell them that they'd been having a row with him. Especially since it was over Holly herself and she was standing right there.

'You're not calling out a helicopter?' asked Colin.

'None available at the moment, I'm afraid. There might be later. Think they've got a coastal search on.'

The team were strapping lights to their foreheads like the ones Holly had seen in a book about coal miners.

'Would I be able to go with you?' asked Colin. 'I'm a doctor, as well as his father. And I know the hills.'

'I'm sorry.' The leader put a hand on his shoulder. 'I know how you feel but we prefer not to have family members –'

'I understand.'

'They might get too worked up, I suppose,' said Holly.

'Especially if they were to find Johnny –' Sylvie stopped.

'What?'

'Well, injured. Or even dead.'

'We mustn't think that!'

But it was too late. They already had.

The men were getting ready to set off, checking their kit with each other and strapping on their rucksacks. The leader explained that they would fan out in groups as they approached the hill so that they could cover as much ground as possible. The police would stay at the roadside and keep in contact with them by radio.

'Good luck!' cried Colin.

Nina didn't say anything. She just stood there, hands locked together in front of her.

They watched as the men headed off up the long undulating path, their headlights bobbing in the darkness. Within seconds they were gone, no longer visible through the rain. Holly shivered. She thought she heard the sound of a whistle. Would Johnny hear it, wherever he was?

'I'm going to take you and Holly home now, Nina,' said Colin. 'It could be a while before there's any news. No point in the two of you hanging around here in the cold. I'll come back and wait with the police.' Nina said nothing, but climbed into the car, her head bowed. Holly followed and they drove back to the cottage in silence.

The wood fire had almost gone out by the time they got in and had to be rekindled. The room, though, was warm still. It would be cold up on the mountain ridge at night.

'Are you hungry, Holly?' Nina asked.

'Not very.'

'No, neither am I, but I think we'd better eat something and keep our strength up. What would you fancy?'

'Beans on toast,' suggested Holly though she didn't know if Nina would like something simple like that.

'Good idea!'

'I could make it.' Holly'd had plenty of practice.

'OK then, if you're willing, go ahead!'

Holly made the toast, heated the beans carefully and served it up to Nina. She also made a pot of tea.

'Thank you, dear. That's kind of you.'

It was black as pitch outside but Nina made no move to close the curtains. They couldn't see anything except the faint wink of a light from a cottage along the road.

They were in the middle of eating when someone knocked on the side window. Nina leapt up at once. It could be news about Johnny! They couldn't make the person out – in fact, there were two of them – so Nina opened the front door and put on the outside light to help the visitors find their way round on the path. Holly went and joined her on the step.

Into view came two people, a man and a woman,

whom Holly had never seen before. And, from the look on Nina's face, neither had she. The woman was leading the way even though she appeared to be limping.

'Nina Nightingale!' she cried. 'It must be! I recognize you from the photograph on your website. We've found you, at last!'

Nina was unable to speak. Holly wasn't surprised. Of course they both guessed at once who the woman must be from her accent. Holly was thinking that maybe it wasn't such a good idea to put your face on a website.

'Mariposa,' said the woman, coming forward with her hand outstretched. Nina took it. It would have been difficult for her not to without being very rude. Mariposa was an exceedingly large woman and she was wearing a voluminous cape that flapped in the wind. 'How lovely to meet you! And this is my husband Bulmer.'

Bulmer grasped Nina's hand between both of his and held on to it for a moment. He looked into her face. 'This means a great deal to my wife, you know. A great deal.'

Nina emerged from her trance. 'How did you find me?'

'We asked at the bookshop in Aviemore. It was Bulmer's idea.' Mariposa smiled proudly at her husband.

'Made sense, didn't it?' He came forward into the light. He was small and thin, in contrast to his wife. 'As I said to Mariposa, if a bookshop can't tell you how to track down a world-famous author, who can?' He had a big, bellowing laugh for such a small man, which Holly found interesting.

'They were terribly kind at the shop, and most helpful,' Mariposa went on. 'Once I explained that we were involved on a project together –'

She got no further before she was cut off.

'We are not involved in anything and you had no right to claim that we are or to come here and invade my privacy.' Nina sounded very severe. 'I'm sorry but I'm afraid I must ask you to leave.'

Surely they would realize they weren't welcome now, thought Holly.

Mariposa took a step back. 'But Evangeline said –'

'Evangeline can say anything she likes as long as you understand that she has not been authorized by me to say it.'

Holly liked the way Nina had put that. So did Sylvie of course.

'Also,' added Nina, 'we have a problem on our hands at the moment. A serious one. My son is lost in the hills.'

'Oh my dear!' cried Mariposa. 'How absolutely dreadful!'

'The Mountain Rescue team are out searching for him.'

'I am so sorry.' Bulmer had started to back away. 'I did wonder if we should have come without an invitation, Mariposa.'

'But Evangeline said –'

'I fear you've been misled.' Nina spoke more quietly this time.

'Let's go, Mariposa,' said her husband. 'I think we'd better.' He took her arm and was about to pull her away when she tipped over on her ankle and went down in a heap on the patio, screaming with pain.

'It's my bad ankle,' she moaned.

'Oh, my goodness,' cried Nina, who had no option but to go out and help Bulmer raise his wife from the ground. Holly hovered, trying to help too but there wasn't much space on the patio between the flower tubs. She was only getting in the way. In addition, Mariposa did not look a light weight.

'Go in and put the kettle on,' advised Sylvie. 'The woman might need a cup of tea.'

Holly darted inside and did just that. Nina and Bulmer half carried, half dragged, a groaning Mariposa into the house. Once they had managed to manipulate her through the doorway they helped her to collapse on to the settee where she lay sprawled, like a beached whale.

'I can't apologize enough, Mrs Nightingale,' said Bulmer. 'Especially troubling you at this difficult time.'

'But we didn't know about that, Bulmer!' wailed Mariposa.

'We shouldn't have come at all. You're right, Mrs Nightingale, we should not have invaded your privacy and landed on you like this.'

'Land is the right word,' commented Sylvie. 'How is Nina going to get rid of them now?'

'Please accept our most sincere apologies and commiserations.' Bulmer pressed Nina's hand between his.

Holly felt kind of sorry for him. He seemed OK really. Mariposa might not be so bad either if she hadn't been led up the garden path by that Evangeline woman. *She* was the pain in the neck. What a nerve she had thinking Nina Nightingale would want to write a book with her friend! Maybe she'd even want to put Sylvie in it. Sylvie said there was no way she'd let anyone else write even a line about her.

'One thing,' observed Sylvie, 'it's taking Nina's mind off Johnny. A bit, at least.'

Mariposa was moaning. She seemed to be genuinely in pain.

'I'm fairly sure you've sprained your ankle,' Nina told her briskly.

As a doctor's wife, she knew what to do. She rang the NHS 24 helpline and explained the problem. Meanwhile, Holly made a pot of tea and served the visitors, who seemed grateful for a hot drink.

Nina finished her call and said an ambulance would come up from Aviemore to collect Mariposa. 'They should be able to bind up your ankle at least and then you can see a doctor in the morning.'

'That's wonderful!' said Bulmer. 'I'll follow it in the hire car.'

'You're so kind,' added Mariposa. 'Evangeline was right. And what a lovely daughter you've got! Is it Holly you're called, darling?'

Holly nodded. She felt she was blushing again. Was she meant to say she wasn't Nina's daughter?

'Say nothing,' advised Sylvie.

Nina smiled for the first time since their guests had arrived. 'She's a good tea-maker. Aren't you, Holly?'

'We've booked into a B&B in Aviemore for a few days,' said Bulmer.

The smile dropped from Nina's face when she heard that.

It wasn't long before the ambulance arrived.

Before being stretchered out Mariposa said, 'You know, Nina, I feel that we do connect. I sense it. I think we will do something together after all. And I shall pray for your son's safe return.'

After Nina had closed the door she started to laugh and Holly joined in.

'Mariposa!' said Nina. 'It means "butterfly" in Spanish. Some butterfly!'

That started them laughing all over again. But once they'd sobered up Holly saw the worry come flooding back into Nina's face.

'You know, Holly,' said Nina, 'I'm very glad you're here to keep me company.'

'Go on, say something in return,' urged Sylvie.

'I like being with you too.' Holly felt suddenly shy.

'Good! So it's mutual. You're getting used to the country too, aren't you, now that you know that there aren't dangerous animals lurking round every corner?'

Holly laughed and Nina smiled.

'We need to do something to occupy ourselves. We can't sit here waiting for the phone to ring. Let's have a go at the jigsaw.'

They worked on it together and Holly gradually found she was getting better at spotting pieces that fitted into different parts of the picture. They both concentrated hard. Nina didn't look at her watch too often, only occasionally, and then she would frown and her eyes become troubled. But she didn't mention Johnny's name or wonder, aloud at least, how they were getting on up there on the dark hill. Holly felt her spine twitch when she thought of it. She eyed the phone sitting silently on its rest and wished it would ring.

'But only for good news,' said Sylvie.

Finally, they slotted the last pieces into the jigsaw. Nina sat back and rubbed her eyes.

It had passed midnight, Holly saw, when she sneaked a look at her watch, but she didn't mention it. It had been a long evening, and it wasn't over yet.

Nina stood up and stretched. She walked to the window and peered out into the darkness.

'At least the sky has cleared and there's a quarter moon.' She sighed. 'It should shed a little light.'

And then the phone rang.

Sixteen

Nina grabbed the receiver.

'Colin, is that you? I can't hear you very well.' She was listening carefully. 'They've found him? Thank goodness! Where?'

Holly ran over to stand beside Nina.

'Damn!' cried Nina.

'What is it?' Holly gulped.

'We got cut off.'

The phone rang again. This time Colin's voice seemed to be clearer.

'On the other side of the ridge, did you say?' asked Nina. 'Is he all right?'

Holly held her breath.

'He'd *fallen*? How far?' Nina had her free hand up to her throat. She looked as if she were going to choke. To Holly, in an aside, she said, 'He isn't going to say of course.' She listened again. 'Not too far? But they think he might have broken his leg? I hope that's *all*!' She closed her eyes for a moment. 'They've got a helicopter coming? That's good anyway. OK, see you soon, love.' She rang off.

'Is he all right?' asked Holly.

'What a stupid question, Holly Hamilton!' scoffed Sylvie. 'How could he be *all* right with a broken leg?'

'Colin wouldn't tell me that Johnny had fallen a

hundred feet down a cliff and was lying unconscious at the bottom, would he?'

Holly shook her head slowly. 'Colin wouldn't want to worry you.'

'They'll take good care of them, though, the men. They're wonderful.'

'Boy in my class broke his leg last year. He's fine now. Back playing footer. I saw him in the street the other day.'

The phone rang again and Nina leapt on it. 'Colin, any more news?' She gave a little smile. 'Thanks.'

'Good news?' asked Holly.

'Colin had forgotten to tell me something. Johnny sent us his love! How could he forget to tell me that!'

'But that means he can speak!'

'Exactly! He must be conscious. Isn't that wonderful?'

And then Nina burst into tears.

Holly had never imagined that it would be *she* who would be comforting a famous writer and not the other way round. She put her arms round Nina like she might do to her own mum when she'd been crying. That was usually after her mum had rowed with Lenny the Louse. The last big row had been when he'd announced he was going to go and live in Bulgaria. Just like that! And he expected Holly's mum to go with him, without a moment's thought. He was full of guff, Sylvie said. For a start, he doesn't even know where Bulgaria is, and for another thing, he didn't have enough money to buy a toffee apple let alone a plane ticket. Holly realized with a shock that she hadn't thought much about her mum in the past couple of days. But she still wondered where she was, and what she was doing. Could she be in Bulgaria, now?

Nina dried her eyes and blew her nose and then she smiled and shook her head. 'It was just the relief of it! Knowing Johnny was actually conscious.'

And sending her and his dad his love, too, thought Holly. That was part of it.

'Would you like a cup of tea?' she asked.

'Maybe not, love. I think I've had enough tea for one day. But Colin might be ready for one when he comes in. He's on his way.'

Holly went off to refill the kettle, her mind was buzzing. Why had Johnny gone up on the ridge on his own when he had been specifically told not to? That was the question that was bothering her. And Nina too, no doubt. Holly couldn't get rid of the idea that Johnny had been wanting to punish them for bringing her into their family and spoiling his holiday. That must be how he saw it. Or at least had chosen to see it.

'It's his own fault if he fell and broke his leg,' stressed Sylvie. 'After all, he shouldn't have gone up there in the first place.'

Holly knew that, but it didn't make her feel any better.

'You've got to stop feeling guilty all the time!' Sylvie was good at lecturing.

Colin came in looking wet and cold as the kettle boiled.

'They'll phone as soon as the helicopter reaches Johnny,' he said. 'No point in heading to the hospital until he's picked up.'

Nina insisted he change his clothes before he drank his tea. She wanted him to eat something too but he wasn't hungry.

The phone rang an hour later. The helicopter had landed and was about to fly Johnny to Raigmore Hospital in Inverness. The three of them ran out into the garden, Holly tagging along behind Nina and Colin.

Shortly afterwards they saw something appear in the sky above the ridge. As it came winging its way down the glen and over their heads it looked, with its vast spotlight, like a huge yellow insect or an object from outer space.

'Let's go,' said Colin. 'The road into Inverness will be quiet at this time of night. Would you mind driving, Nina?'

☆ ☆ ☆

It took them only forty minutes to drive up the A9 to the hospital.

They went first to Reception and were told that Johnny had arrived and was being examined. Colin explained that he was a doctor and the nurse ushered him off.

Nina and Holly sat in a waiting room with three or four other people, all of whom looked gloomy and dead tired. It wasn't surprising since it was the middle of the night. Holly was finding it difficult to keep awake herself. This was the first time she had ever actually been inside a hospital. She'd only seen them on television when they had emergencies on their hands and were rushing up and down corridors pushing trolleys with ill people laid out on them.

It was very still in here. No one was rushing anywhere. And it was warm. Holly's head drooped and before she knew it she was asleep.

She was wakened by Nina gently shaking her shoulder and for a moment she couldn't think where she was.

'Wake up, Holly. We're going to go and see Johnny.'

They walked quietly along the corridors and a nurse pointed them in the right direction.

Johnny was in a room on his own. Nina went straight in but Holly hung back in the corridor. He wouldn't want to see her, he'd want his mum and dad. That was only natural. He'd never liked her anyway. Sylvie knew that was true so she kept quiet.

'Are you all right, dear?' asked a nurse, passing along the corridor.

'Fine, thank you.'

'Are you the boy's sister?'

Holly shook her head.

'You're with them though?'

'Yes.'

'Why don't you go in?'

'I'm OK here.'

'You can go in if you want to,' said the nurse before moving on.

Holly could see through the side window into the room. Johnny was lying back against a heap of pillows with his head bandaged. So he had hit his head too! His parents were on either side of the bed, sitting in very close to it, and him. His mother had her hand on his arm and she was talking. Holly looked away. She felt as if she were snooping. This wasn't a time to listen in. They'd forgotten all about her. That was to be expected, said Sylvie. He was their son, after all. And he had been fairly seriously injured.

The same nurse came back along. 'Still here? You can't stand in the corridor all night. Are you related to the family?'

'No.'

'But you are with them?'

'Yes.'

'Just a friend then?'

'Yes.' Just a friend.

'I'm sure it would be all right if you did go in, you know.'

Holly was saved from further cross-examination by the arrival of a doctor. He gave her no more than a passing glance and went sweeping into Johnny's room, followed by the nurse. They shut the door.

Holly wandered further along the corridor and met another nurse, who also asked if she could help her.

'Are you looking for somebody?'

'I'm waiting for Johnny's mum and dad. Mr and Mrs Nightingale,' Holly added. She felt awkward, calling them that. She was used to thinking of them as Nina and Colin now.

'Oh, I see.' The nurse nodded. 'Is the doctor in with them?'

She seemed satisfied when she was told that he was and carried on.

Holly wished she had a book with her. She hung

around and every time a nurse or someone in a white coat appeared she had to answer the same set of questions. One or two gave her a suspicious look as if she'd no right to be there at all.

Eventually the doctor emerged and shortly afterwards a man with a trolley appeared at the end of the corridor and wheeled it into Johnny's room. Five minutes later the trolley came out again with Johnny lying on top. His father followed. And then came Nina.

She turned, saw Holly and came over to her.

'Holly love, there you are!' She put her arm round Holly's shoulder. 'You should have come in.'

'I didn't like to.'

'You could have done.'

Holly couldn't help feeling happy – it was clear that Nina meant it, and that she was pleased to see her.

'How's Johnny?'

'He was suffering from hypothermia when they found him –' Nina broke off to say, by way of explanation for Holly, 'That's when someone has been exposed to severe cold. But he wasn't too bad, considering he'd been out on the hill for so long. He was warmly dressed, fortunately!'

'So where has he gone now?'

'To X-Ray. You and I will go and find the café and have a drink of something. It must be nearly breakfast-time.'

Holly had hot chocolate and Nina a cup of coffee. She also bought some croissants.

'Is Johnny going to be all right?'

'They're not sure about the break until they do the X-rays. But it doesn't look good. He bashed his head too but they think it's just cut and bruised. It could have been worse. He did fall quite a way apparently.'

Holly supposed he might have killed himself.

They stayed in the café until Colin joined them. He also had a cup of coffee and ate a croissant in about thirty seconds.

'I needed that!'

'Have they done the X-ray?' asked Nina.

He nodded. 'Unfortunately, it's a fairly complicated break. They'll be taking him into theatre quite soon to set it. It's going to be a little tricky.'

'Oh no!'

'Don't start worrying now! I expect it'll be OK in the end – he's young after all. His bones have a better chance of mending than ours would.'

'That's true.' Nina seemed a little comforted, though not much.

'It'll take time of course and he won't be running around or playing any sports for a while.'

'He won't like that. You know what he's like when he can't get out and about.'

'He'll just have to thole it.' That was exactly what Holly was thinking.

'He's survived,' his father went on, 'and that's the main thing. He'll probably be kept in for a day or two so I'll stay up here with him and you can go back to the house with Holly, Nina. Cousin Jack will put me up.'

It was because of her that Nina wouldn't be able to stay in Inverness with her son, Holly knew. They could hardly take a stranger to stay at Cousin Jack's.

'I'm just a nuisance to you,' she said.

'No, you're not,' protested Colin.

'Listen, Holly,' said Nina, reaching out to touch her hand, 'I don't know what I'd have done without you. I'd have gone round the bend last night if I'd been on my own waiting for news.'

'Is that true?'

'It certainly is!' Nina looked Holly straight in the face. 'And you're a great tea-maker!'

Holly smiled.

Nina decided that she and Holly should go for a walk while Colin waited at the hospital. He would ring her once Johnny was back in the ward.

Nina drove Holly and herself into the centre of Inverness and parked by the river. They walked along the path and then sat on a seat in a pool of early morning sunlight, watching a group of green-backed ducks swimming lazily by. They were mallard ducks, Nina told Holly.

'I saw some like that when my dad took me to Loch Lomond.'

'You must have enjoyed that?'

'Oh I did! We went out on a boat. He always takes me to really nice places and we have a lovely meal afterwards.'

'You're very fond of your dad, aren't you?'

Holly nodded. She had the lump in her throat again when she thought of him. And her mum, too, but she was trying not to think about her at present for she was still cross with her.

They were quiet for a while and then Holly asked,

'Have you ever been to Bulgaria?'

'Bulgaria?' Nina seemed surprised. 'No, I haven't. Why, have you?'

'No, I was just wondering. You could write a book about Sylvie going to Bulgaria?'

'I'd need to go there first though, wouldn't I?'

'Couldn't you make it up? From pictures and things. My mum's got a whole stack of holiday catalogues.'

'No, I wouldn't do that. I'd need to know a place well before I'd write about it. It wouldn't ring true if I didn't.'

'Suppose not.'

Another silence, broken this time by Nina.

'Have you got a special interest in Bulgaria, Holly?'

Holly shrugged.

'Do you think that might be where your mum's gone on holiday?'

'Might.'

'Well, we'll just have to wait until she comes back to find out, won't we?' said Nina cheerfully.

'*If* she comes back,' put in Sylvie, echoing Holly's thoughts.

Seventeen

Johnny arrived back in the glen in an ambulance three days later, his leg encased in a plaster cast from the thigh to just below the knee. He would have to wear it for six weeks and was already complaining about that. The surgeon was pleased, however, with the way the operation had gone and hopeful that there would be no permanent damage to the leg.

He managed to hobble up the garden, using his crutches – he insisted. His mother kept a short distance behind him, taking care not to fuss too much. Holly could see that she kept wanting to put her arms out to catch him in case he fell over.

They got him into the house and settled him on the settee.

It was plain that Johnny was going to enjoy being an invalid. He wanted a cup of coffee and then changed his mind, he'd have hot chocolate and a ham sandwich and, as an afterthought, a cheese one as well. He was starving. The food in the hospital had been rubbish, he claimed. He wanted a glass of water.

He wanted attention.

'Perhaps he deserves it,' said Sylvie. 'At least for a while.'

After all, he had had a nasty time. He must have wondered whether he might die out there in the hills, and the pain in his leg had been fierce. Holly had to admit that he seemed to have coped well with all of it. It was rotten of her but she couldn't help feeling sorry he was back though. She'd had a lovely time with Nina on their own in the evenings after they'd come back from visiting Johnny. They'd talked about all sorts of things, but books mostly, and Nina had told her how she'd started to write.

'I loved reading when I was a child, just like you, Holly, and I could never get enough to read. So one day, when I was moaning in my mum's ear about having nothing to read she said to me, "Why don't you go and write a book of your own?"'

'So you did?'

'I got lined, foolscap paper and filled my fountain pen with green ink because I thought that would be an artistic colour to use!'

They'd laughed.

'So I wrote my first book. I was eleven years old. Same age as you, Holly. You could write a book if you wanted.'

Holly had gone to bed thinking about that.

Now that Johnny was back, she decided she should stay out of everybody's way for a bit, so she went to her room and took out her notebook. She wrote up some notes about all the things that had been happening to her.

It was so chilly in the unheated room, that her hands were gradually becoming numb. After a while she ventured back to the sitting room, hoping she wouldn't be noticed. As she opened the door she heard Johnny's voice.

'I'm surprised she's still here,' he was saying.

Holly froze.

'Don't refer to Holly as *she*, please!' his mother retorted. 'I've told you before.'

'I thought you'd have got rid of her by now.'

'Be quiet!' demanded his father. He lowered his voice. 'She might hear you.'

'Dad called her *she*,' cried Johnny triumphantly.

'I do also call her by her name,' Colin said, mildly.

'And you will have to accept that Holly is going to be with us for the rest of our time here,' added his mother.

Johnny groaned. 'We could have asked Tim's mum if she'd let him come up to keep me company. What am I going to do lying here? We don't even have a telly.'

'Read,' said his mother.

'I can't read all day.'

'We could have a family game of Monopoly,' said his father.

'You always used to say you hated Monopoly when you were forced to play it.'

'It seems I've changed my mind.'

'Well, I haven't,' said Johnny. 'It's a kid's game. For five year olds.'

'We've got loads of jigsaws,' put in his mother.

'Jigsaws!' snorted Johnny.

Holly closed the door quietly and tiptoed back to her room. She crept under the downie.

'Pity they didn't keep him longer at the hospital,' commented Sylvie.

Sometime later there came a tap on the door.

'Can I come in?' asked Nina.

'Uh-huh,' said Holly. For once, Sylvie held her tongue.

Nina opened the door. 'What are you doing in there, love?'

'I just thought maybe Johnny –'

Nina interrupted her. 'Come through to the warm! You're not going to lie in here all day.'

'But Johnny doesn't like me.'

'That's silly.'

'No, it's not. I know he doesn't.' Holly sat up. 'He doesn't like me being here.'

'Well, you are staying and that is that! And Colin and I like you. We do! Very much.' Nina sighed and sat down on the edge of the bed. 'Johnny's just being rather difficult. He's broken his leg –'

'I know and I'm sorry about that.'

'And he'd wanted to bring his friend Tim –'

'And it's 'cos of me he couldn't!'

'Yes, OK, let's face it, that is true,' admitted Nina. 'No point in me trying to deny it. But none of us can get what we want in life all the time. You know that, don't you?'

She put her arm round Holly. 'Just hang in there and don't let Johnny get you down. Let anything he says roll over you. He'll adjust. OK?'

'I'll try.'

'Come on then! Up you get! We're going to play Monopoly, all four of us, whether we like it or not.'

'I thought you wanted to get on with your book?'

'Well, maybe I did. But sometimes more important things get in the way.'

They played Monopoly for the next two hours. They had the Scottish version and Johnny was triumphant when he managed to buy both Edinburgh and Stirling Castles. He was triumphant too when he won in the end. Holly had never played the game before, but she grasped the idea quickly and by the time they were halfway through she found she was beginning to enjoy it.

'Can we play another time?' she asked.

'Yes,' said Nina. 'But not today.'

'Definitely not today,' agreed Colin.

'I must go into the butcher's in Kingussie to buy something for dinner,' said Nina. 'Do you want to come with me, Holly?'

'Yes, please!'

Colin had a few chores to do outside. For a start he wanted to finish chopping his logs.

'You're always chopping logs,' grumped Johnny, back to being sulky again. 'I wish I had my iPod!'

They'd not been able to find it anywhere in the house. Johnny thought he might have had it in his pocket when he'd set off up the ridge, though he couldn't remember exactly. His memory was hazy about the whole incident, due perhaps to the bang he'd got on his head when he fell. Or else, as his mother suspected, he was choosing not to remember so that he wouldn't have to answer any questions. Nina and Colin had decided not to cross-question him or rail on about it. They hoped he'd learned his lesson.

'What about a game of Patience?' proposed his father, a little wickedly, Holly thought. 'You can do that on your own. Or Sudoku?'

Johnny chose Sudoku.

Nina drove the seven miles to Kingussie, where she visited the butcher, the chemist and the grocer. Holly helped to carry the shopping. She tripped happily along beside Nina, chattering about *Anne of Green Gables*.

'You like Anne, do you?' asked Nina. 'Do you feel she's a bit like you?'

'I'm not an orphan,' said Holly quickly. 'I've got a mum and dad.'

'No, I didn't mean that,' returned Nina equally swiftly though Holly wasn't entirely convinced. 'Of course you've got a mum and dad! But Anne's good at making the best of things?'

'Like Sylvie.'

Nina nodded.

When they arrived back at the house they saw a car parked outside their gate.

'Wonder who that can be,' said Nina. 'Looks like a rented car.'

As they passed the side windows they looked into the room. Sitting on the settee were Mariposa and Bulmer. Nina exploded.

'Don't tell me Colin invited them in!'

'Maybe he couldn't stop them.'

'I doubt if they'd actually barge past.'

They went inside.

'We've got visitors,' hissed Colin, cutting them off in the hall.

'We saw the car outside,' said Holly.

'Why did you ask them in?'

'They came to enquire about Johnny.'

Nina didn't look as if she believed that. 'You could have told them and then sent them packing.'

'They wanted to wait till you came back to thank you. What could I do?'

'Tell them I'd gone to Bulgaria with Holly.'

Holly giggled.

'You'd better come in,' said Colin.

They went. Bulmer rose to meet them but Mariposa, who was spread-eagled in a deep armchair, with her bandaged ankle propped on a stool, was unable to get up.

'Nina darling,' she cried, holding out her hand.

Nina was forced to lean over to take it.

'And Holly!' cried Mariposa. 'Your delightful daughter.'

Johnny's eyes goggled. 'She didn't tell you she was their daughter, did she? What a cheek!'

'No, Johnny,' his mother said quietly, 'she did not.'

Mariposa was looking perplexed.

'Holly is a close friend of the family,' explained Nina.

'Oh, I see. She makes the most wonderful pot of tea. We've brought you some chocolates. Just a little thank you to you and Holly for your kindness. Have you got them in the bag, Bulmer?'

Bulmer brought the bag over to the settee. Mariposa took out a box of peppermint creams and handed it to Holly. Then she dug into the bag and produced a bulging folder which she presented to Nina.

'That's for you, darling. I think you'll be enchanted once you get into it.'

Holly eyed Nina. She looked as if she really was going to explode this time.

'She should bung it straight on the fire,' said Sylvie. 'That'd teach Mariposa.'

Nina stood in the middle of the floor holding the folder, making no attempt to open it. 'I take it this is your manuscript?'

'Indeed! What else?'

'I have already told you…' Nina began in a controlled voice.

'Why doesn't she just yell blue murder?' said Sylvie.

Why was it 'blue murder', Holly wondered. Red would seem a more suitable colour. Maybe the idea was to yell until you turned blue in the face?

'I think you might change your mind,' Mariposa was saying, 'if you would just give it a chance.'

You never knew, thought, Holly, it might be good. Sylvie didn't agree. 'No way!'

'I haven't got time,' Nina started again.

'We can leave it with you.'

'That's an idea.' Colin jumped in. 'If you do that we can return it to you once Nina has read it. Where did you say your B&B was?'

Bulmer gave him the address.

'I'm sorry to have to rush you now,' said Colin, 'but I've just remembered that we're due at friends' in a few minutes and it will take us some time to get Johnny into the car.'

He went to the settee and gave Mariposa his hand. Bulmer joined him and together they pulled her into an upright position on her feet.

'What a pity we couldn't have had longer together, Nina dear,' said Mariposa. 'Another time! Evangeline will be delighted to know that we have made contact.'

The two men escorted her out of the house and up the garden. It was slow going.

'I thought you were going to have a fit, Mum,' said Johnny.

'So did I!' Nina flung the folder on to the table. 'If she turns up another time she has got to be stopped before she gets as far as the front door.'

Johnny was sprawled on the settee. He had been doing a crossword in the newspaper.

'How's it going?' asked his mother.

'Just got a couple to get.'

'Johnny's good at crosswords,' Nina told Holly.

'A small boat,' he read out. 'Begins with the letter "c".'

'Canoe,' said Nina immediately.

'Doesn't fit.'

'How many letters?'

'Seven.'

'Seven?' Nina frowned.

'Coracle,' suggested Holly hesitantly, not sure if she should have butted in.

'Coracle?' repeated Johnny. 'What on earth's that?'

'Holly's right, it's a small boat,' said Nina. 'A rowing boat. It's made of skin. Welsh, I believe?'

'Think so,' said Holly, feeling a little embarrassed.

'Does it fit?'

Johnny pursed his mouth. 'Seems to,' he muttered as he pencilled in the letters.

He wasn't pleased to find that she knew something he didn't, thought Holly.

'How did you know that, love?' asked Nina.

'I read it in a book that my dad bought me.'

The door opened to admit Colin. He looked hot in the face.

'Now don't start!' He held up his hand. 'I will return the manuscript tomorrow to their B&B. I had to get rid of them somehow.'

'And if she ever turns up here again,' said Nina, 'tell her that I have gone to Bulgaria and am not coming back!'

She turned and grinned at Holly.

Eighteen

Holly wasn't sure if she should have spoken out in the way she had. Johnny hadn't liked her knowing the answer when he didn't. He'd been surprised, too. He probably thought she was stupid, just because her mother wasn't a famous children's writer and her father wasn't a doctor. Perhaps she should have kept her mouth closed.

Lenny the Louse told her to shut it at times and called her 'Little Miss Know-All.' She knew a lot more than he did anyway. That wasn't hard. Her mum said (when he wasn't there) to ignore him when he was in a mumpy mood. She was proud that Holly stuck in at her lessons. She wished she had done so herself. Then she wouldn't have to work nights in the *Silver Spike*. She'd been silly and mitched school and got into trouble.

'I don't want you going down that route, pet,' she'd said.

Holly had no intention of going there. It didn't sound like a good route to her. She actually *liked* going to school. Some of the girls in her class thought she was nuts but she didn't care. She'd have hated to sit in the house on her own or to hang about in a cold street pretending she was having a good time.

'I think Lenny wishes he'd done better at school too,' Holly's mum had added. 'He could have done OK, you know, if he'd stuck in.'

Holly wasn't convinced about that. She thought he was as thick as a plank and Sylvie agreed.

'He's just jealous,' Holly's mum had said, 'when you show him up.'

Holly didn't want Johnny to be jealous of her. Sylvie warned her to be careful then and not do annoying things like shout out an answer in his crossword before he had a chance to get it himself.

'But he didn't know "coracle"!' protested Holly. 'And I didn't shout it out. I waited.'

She heeded Sylvie's advice though next morning when Johnny was doing the crossword in that day's paper. She concentrated on her book. From time to time she lifted her head and took a quick look at him. More than once she saw him frowning. She was dying to ask if she could help.

'Don't!' warned Sylvie. 'You've got to be nice to him. He's an invalid, remember!'

They were alone in the room. Colin had gone to town to buy something in the hardware store and Nina was working in the garden.

Johnny broke the silence.

'Alternatively,' he said.

'Alternatively? How many letters?'

'Two and four.'

Holly thought, then said, 'Or else?'

'Of course!' He wrote it in. 'Here's one you'll know since you read so much. The island where a red-headed girl called Anne lived. Six and six.'

'That's easy-peasy! Prince Edward. It's in *Anne of Green Gables*. I've just been reading it.'

'I thought you'd know that. Sounded like a girl's book. Where is it anyway?'

'Canada. I've seen it on the map. I'm going to go there one day and see Anne's house. It's white and green and made of wood.'

She'd love to go with Nina!

'You never know!' said Sylvie. She was an optimist. Holly had made a note of the word 'optimist' after reading it in one of Nina's books.

Johnny printed PRINCE EDWARD in the empty boxes and nodded.

'How's it going?' asked Holly.

'Not bad. Just a few to get. Bit stuck on a couple.' He hesitated. 'Want to have a look?'

Holly pulled a chair over to the settee and between them they managed to finish the crossword quite quickly. Johnny was going to do a Sudoku next. His father had bought him a thick book of puzzles.

'That should keep you quiet for a while,' he'd said.

'Could you show me how you do Sudoku?' asked Holly.

'That's a good idea,' approved Sylvie, 'asking for his help. Smart.'

'I've never tried before,' added Holly.

Johnny seemed quite pleased to be asked and worked his way slowly through the puzzle, explaining each move to her as he went along.

'Do *you* want to have a go?' he asked when he'd finished it. 'Here's one graded "Easy".' He passed her his pencil with the rubber on the end.

Holly glanced up to find Nina peeping through the back window. Nina smiled and moved away.

Holly soon realized how essential the rubber was! She made several mistakes but each time Johnny intervened and told her where she was going wrong. When she finally got all the numbers lined up in their proper order she felt pleased with herself.

'That wasn't bad,' said Johnny.

'Big praise,' said Sylvie.

'I couldn't have done it without you. How's your leg?' Holly looked at Johnny's plaster cast. A number of people at the hospital had written their signatures on it and he'd asked his parents to do add theirs, but he hadn't asked her. 'Is it still awful sore?'

He made a face. 'When I move it the wrong way it hurts. I'm still having to take painkillers. Don't want to but I have to.'

'It was bad luck doing that when you were on holiday.'

'You're telling me!'

The door opened to admit Nina, who had come to make drinks for them all. Holly moved her chair away from the settee and went to put the kettle on.

After lunch Johnny asked his father if he would give him a game of chess.

'Maybe later,' said Colin.

'Why not now?'

'I have to go to Inverness this afternoon. Jack lent me his special spanner and I must take it back.'

'You're going all that way to take a spanner back?'

'I am.'

Johnny was sulking again. He looked in his mother's direction. 'What about you, Mum?'

'You know I don't play chess!'

'You could try.'

'No, I couldn't. I've told you before. I've got enough going on in my life without adding chess to the list.'

That left Holly.

Johnny turned towards her, but she shrank back reluctantly.

'He's bored,' said Sylvie. 'He doesn't like playing Patience and he's had enough of crosswords and Sudoku puzzles for one day. Don't blame him.'

'I don't know how to play chess,' said Holly. She didn't fancy trying to learn either, from what she knew about it. She'd rather go out and help Nina in the garden, for then they could chat about books.

'It's bit like draughts,' put in Nina.

'Mother!' Johnny was indignant. 'Like draughts! It is not. It's ten times more difficult.'

That was what Holly was afraid of.

'You think you'll be rubbish at it, don't you?' put in Sylvie. 'And then he'll smirk.'

'You could teach Holly, Johnny,' said Colin.

'I don't think…' Holly backed away.

'Go on, give it a go!' urged Colin. 'Clever girl like you will pick it up in no time.'

'Don't be bullied into it, though, Holly,' said Nina. 'Only do it if you want to.'

What was Holly to do now? They were all waiting to find out.

Sylvie thought she might like it. 'You never know, do you, till you try? It would be one in the eye for loopy old Lenny the Louse if you told him you could play chess.'

That swayed Holly. She agreed.

'Be patient now, Johnny,' cautioned his mother. 'Remember that Holly is a total beginner. You can't expect her to pick it up in ten minutes.'

She fetched the chess set from a cupboard.

'You're sure now?' she asked Holly.

Holly nodded. Johnny was unpacking the chess men already.

Nina went back to her gardening, Colin took off for Inverness. Holly sat down and faced Johnny across the chess board.

'Now,' he began, 'these little ones are called pawns…'

Three hours later Holly staggered out into the garden, desperate for some fresh air. Her head felt as if it were going to burst.

'How did you get on?' Nina was resting on a garden chair round the back of the house, a book open on her lap, her face tilted towards the sun.

'I was rubbish.'

'I don't believe that.'

'My head's thumping.'

'You've played too long. I should have come in and stopped you but I got carried away and forgot the time.'

Holly squatted on a flat stone beside Nina and they got to talking about L.M.Montgomery, the author of *Anne of Green Gables*. Nina had some of her other books that she'd kept since she was a child, with titles that appealed to Holly like *Emily of Lantern Hill* and *Rilla of Ingleside*. Nina said she'd lend them to her.

'I'll be very careful with them,' promised Holly.

'I know you will.'

'I never turn over the corners of pages.'

'That's a horrible thing to do to books, isn't it?' said Nina.

They were in agreement about that. Also about opening a book and placing the pages face downward so that the spine tended to split.

When they went back inside they found Johnny asleep on the settee.

'You've exhausted him!' Nina whispered, smiling. 'He still needs a lot of rest.'

They tiptoed back out without waking him and went for a walk in the wood.

A deer ran in front of them but Holly didn't jump this time. She loved the quiet, graceful way it moved.

'It was good of you to play chess with Johnny,' said Nina. 'He'll be pestering you to play again! He's mad about chess.'

'I don't mind.' Holly realized that she didn't. She'd actually enjoyed the game once she'd begun to get the hang of it.

After that she and Johnny played chess together every day and gradually she found herself becoming more and more interested. She even managed to win a couple of times but she knew Johnny had more or less let her, though he denied it, which, as Sylvie said, was nice of him. He only called her an idiot once when she made a stupid move.

And, on the second day, when they had finished playing, he asked her in an off-hand sort of way if she'd like to sign his cast.

'Don't mind,' she said and, as neatly as she could on the uneven white surface, signed her name in blue ink, '*Holly Hamilton*'.

Nineteen

Johnny began to hobble around on his crutches. He was bored lying on the settee and nobody could blame him. Nina watched carefully over him, especially when he went outside. She wouldn't let him go into the wood.

'Why not? Just a little way!'

'That path's far too uneven. You could easily trip. We don't want any more accidents and I'm tired of driving up and down to hospital in Inverness.'

'I second that,' said his father.

Johnny was much less moody now though, since he'd become at least semi-mobile. But after a short outing he was glad to get back to his couch and collapse.

'When will I ever be able to play rugger again? Or footer? Or anything?'

'It takes time,' was all his father could say, which always raised a groan from Johnny.

Every day, however, for some period of time, it was peaceful in the house when Johnny and Holly were deep into their game of chess.

'Holly, you've been fantastic with Johnny,' Nina said when they were out in the garden on their own. 'I don't know what we would have done without you. The two of you seem to have become good friends, which is great.'

Holly wondered whether they'd be quite such good friends in Edinburgh.

She hadn't thinking much about going back in Edinburgh. Or Glasgow. For the last few days she hadn't been thinking ahead at all. She liked being here, away from Lenny the Louse and the old bag that lived in the next stair and was always trying to find fault with her mum. She liked being with Nina and Colin. She even quite liked Johnny! Though she knew of course that he would prefer to be with Tim or Mike if he had the choice. But at least he had stopped moaning about not being able to have his pals here.

'It's only natural he'd want to be with his own friends,' said Sylvie. 'He'll be back with them again soon and then he won't have time for you.' There were times when Holly wished that her friend wasn't quite so full of opinions.

Nina had wandered off round the garden so Holly slipped out of the gate and went a little way into the wood. Nina had warned her not to go far on her own.

Sylvie had made her think. She couldn't go on pretending that life here at the cottage would go on forever. They were due to leave the glen on Friday, in two days' time. The second week of the holiday had flown past. Only two more days left!

'Now you don't want to leave here, do you?' said Sylvie.

Two weeks ago, Holly didn't even want to venture into the woods with Nina. Here she was, happily walking up the track on her own, able to name the flowers and trees, and no longer worried about wolves coming to gobble her up.

'Everything's going to change again,' said Sylvie.

Holly really didn't need reminding. On Saturday her dad should be back in Edinburgh and her mum in Glasgow. *Should* be. If they managed not to miss their planes or forget to collect her. On Saturday her life should be back to normal, whatever that was.

☆　☆　☆

'You know Nina thinks your mum is irresponsible,' said Sylvie the following day. 'And isn't fit to bring you up. You heard her say so to Colin, didn't you?'

Nina had been talking to Colin in the garden and she hadn't realized that Johnny had opened the sitting room window to let a bee out.

'Fancy putting her on a train with a woman she'd never clapped eyes on!' Nina had said.

'That was you!'

'Yes, I know, but it could have been anyone. She just wanted rid of Holly.'

'That's not true!' Holly said, squirming. 'She didn't want rid of me.'

'It was true at that moment, though. She had to get you on the train to Edinburgh somehow.' Whose side was Sylvie on?

'But it didn't mean that she wanted rid of me forever.'

'I never said that!'

'If only she would get rid of Lenny!'

'Even if she did she'd go on working at the *Spike* every night. She likes it, doesn't she? All her friends are there.

She doesn't like being cooped up in the house. She gets restless.'

Nina and Colin were still talking outside.

'It's not up to us to decide what her mum's fit for, Nina,' Colin had said.

'I realize that but I can't bear the thought of her being all alone in the evening while her mother's out at work. It's simply not fair!'

'I agree. But I don't know what we can do about it.'

'I've got very fond of her, Colin. I'll miss her. I wish —'

'We can't have her to live with us, love,' Colin had said quietly. 'She's got parents of her own.'

At that point, they had moved away and Holly heard no more.

'You've got fond of Nina too, haven't you?' Sylvie said now. 'But you love your mum.'

'Course.'

'You don't really fancy being back in the flat on your own at nights though, do you?'

'I won't be on my own. I'll be with you.'

'Not quite the same though, is it? Not like being with the three of them here?'

Holly was silent. She couldn't kid herself that it was the same, talking to a voice in her head, even if it was Sylvie's voice. It wasn't the same as talking to Nina and Colin, or even Johnny. Yes, even Johnny. She had to admit it.

She hoped Nina and Colin wouldn't go to the Social Services and tell them her mum wasn't fit to bring her up. She didn't think they would. She trusted them not to. But they might tell her dad.

'Very likely,' agreed Sylvie.

And then what?

'You can't live with him, can you?' said Sylvie. 'He lives on an oil rig half the time. They don't allow children on oil rigs.'

'I know that,' said Holly, biting her fingernail.

'But you can't expect to stay on with Nina and Colin, can you?'

'I'm *not* expecting to,' snapped Holly though at times during the past week she had allowed herself to have a little daydream about it. But after a bit her mum and then her dad would appear in her dream and it would come apart. The whole thing had become too much to think about so she had shoved it to the back of her head. Until now.

☆　☆　☆

Friday morning arrived and they had to pack up to go back south.

'I wish we could stay longer,' Nina said to Holly, 'but holidays can't last forever. Though you might be lucky enough to have another one with your dad?'

'The school doesn't like you staying off.'

'No – and quite right too. But in the circumstances, perhaps if your dad were to explain, they might let you. You must be looking forward to seeing him?'

Holly nodded. She *was* looking forward to seeing him but what if he didn't turn up again? There'd been no further word from him. That was was understandable. Colin had given him their Edinburgh number, not the cottage one, and their mobiles seldom got a signal in the glen. He had left a message the previous weekend to to tell her dad that Holly was fine, and when they expected to be back in Edinburgh, but he hadn't been available for Holly to talk to.

'I expect he'll ring when he gets into Edinburgh on Saturday,' said Nina.

'Let's hope,' put in Sylvie.

'If not,' added Nina, 'you can stay with us until he does. So don't worry about it. Want to give me a hand with my stuff? You could take the laptop if you like?'

Holly carried it carefully.

'You didn't get to do much writing,' she said.

'No, I didn't! Too much going on.'

'That's a shame.'

'I'll catch up. There'll be peace and quiet when everyone is back at work and school.'

'Did you ever read Mariposa's story?'

'I had a look at it.'

'Is it any good?'

'As a matter of fact it's not bad!' Nina laughed.

'You're not going to write a book with her though, are you?'

'No, but I'll write her a note and give her my comments.'

They hadn't seen any more of Mariposa and Bulmer. Sylvie thought Bulmer had probably persuaded his wife not to trouble them again.

Johnny would travel back with Colin in the car. He

would take up the whole of the rear seat with his plaster cast, which would leave only the front seat free. So Nina and Holly were to go by train.

Colin ran them to the station in Aviemore before returning to pick up Johnny. Nina told him they would take a taxi when they got into Edinburgh.

'Are you sure?'

'No point in you coming down to the station. You can get Johnny into the house and sorted out. It might be best for him to sleep downstairs till he gets the cast off.'

'Leave it to me!'

'It's good that's he a doctor,' observed Holly after they'd waved Colin off.

'It has its uses!' Nina smiled.

The train, which had come in from Inverness, looked busy but a number of passengers with huge rucksacks got off at Aviemore. Nina and Holly found two empty window seats and settled in. Holly remembered the last time she'd been on a train with Nina. It seemed like years ago. But it was only two weeks to the day. She wondered if Nina was thinking about it too.

They had a table to themselves and each had a book so sometimes they read and sometimes they talked.

'I like going on journeys,' said Holly. 'You've taken Sylvie on a lot of journeys in your books.'

'I have, haven't I? Where do you think we should go next?'

'What about Prince Edward Island?'

Nina laughed. 'That would be exciting, wouldn't it?'

They went back to their books.

☆ ☆ ☆

The train arrived in Waverley Station right on schedule. They queued for a taxi and were soon whirling through the streets of Edinburgh to the Nightingales' house. The last stage of their journey. They didn't talk now. Holly was feeling a little queasy. When she looked up Nina gave her an encouraging smile and reached out to squeeze her hand.

Nina paid off the taxi driver and opened the gate. When they were halfway up the drive the front door opened and Colin appeared on the doorstep.

'Holly – your dad has just phoned,' he said.

Twenty

Holly couldn't speak for a moment. Her voice croaked when it came back.

'Where is he?' she cried.

'Edinburgh,' said Colin.

'In his flat?'

'Yes.'

'I knew he'd phone!'

'Oh you did, did you?' Sylvie teased her.

'He actually came back a couple of days early and tried us then.'

'But we were away!'

'He'd got the message. I said I'd ring him as soon as you came in. Let's go into Nina's study and do it from there.'

Colin spoke to Holly's dad first and then handed over the receiver. Her hand shook as she took it. Colin left her alone in the room and closed the door.

'Is that you, Dad?' she gulped.

'Aye, it is. Is that you, Holly?'

'Yes, it is. It's me.' She didn't know whether to laugh or cry.

'Are you all right?'

'Uh-uh.'

'Are you sure? You don't sound all right?'

'No, I am,' she cried. 'I am all right.'

'Those people been good to you?'

'Yes.'

'No trouble at all?'

'No, no trouble. They're great, dad. You'd like them. You really would.'

'Listen, pet, I'm coming over to fetch you right away. I've rented a car. You get your stuff together. Mr Nightingale's given me his address. I'll be there in no more than twenty minutes.'

Holly replaced the receiver. Her head was in a whirl.

She went out into the hall and bumped into Johnny.

'My dad's coming to get me in twenty minutes,' she said. She felt slightly stunned.

'Twenty minutes?' repeated Johnny. 'So *soon*? We haven't finished our chess game. We were going to do it tonight. I'd written down where we were in it.'

Holly looked round and saw Nina. She was standing very still.

'Your dad's on his way, is he, Holly? He must stay and have a cup of tea with us though. We can't let you run away that quickly!'

Holly didn't want to run away. Not *run*. She was trying to get her head round the idea that her dad would actually be here in twenty minutes to take her away.

She'd loved living with the Nightingales once she'd settled in. She'd been happy with them and she would miss them. Nina most of all, of course. But Colin and Johnny too.

Everything seemed to be happening too fast. She couldn't think straight.

'You want to be with your dad though, don't you?' said Sylvie.

'Of course!'

Holly's bags stood by the door. There had been no need to unpack. Nina had given her an extra one for the clothes she'd bought her, the sweat shirts and fleeces and jeans that she'd needed for their holiday in the country. Now there was nothing to do but wait for her dad. Johnny hobbled off to the kitchen.

Holly's dad was true to his word. Twenty minutes later he was on the doorstep ringing the bell. Nina and Colin retreated to the kitchen, leaving Holly to meet him on her own.

'It's great to see you, pet,' he said, opening up his arms to her.

She flew into them and he held her tight. He wasn't a particularly big man but he was broad and he felt safe. He hugged her close and she felt tears welling up in her eyes. She hadn't realized that she'd be so pleased to see him.

'You've nothing to worry about now, Holly love. I'm here to look after you.' After a few seconds he let her go, but still held her by the shoulders, looking her straight in the eye. 'You're not going back to your old life. I won't have it!'

Holly was taken aback by the way he spoke to her – he was almost in tears himself. 'What are you going to do?' she said.

'I've been to the *Spike*,' her dad went on. 'I talked to a friend of your mum's.'

'Chrissie?'

'Aye. She told me about your mum putting you on the train to Edinburgh and all that. She'd no right doing that. She didn't know that this writer woman would bring you home with her, did she?'

'Mum thought you'd be there.'

'That mix-up wasne my fault, love.'

'I know that. Mum hadn't checked your last email, you see. The one where you said your leave was changed.'

'That mother of yours is a piece of rubbish.'

'She's not, Dad. She's OK.'

'She's not fit to be a mother.'

'Don't say that! She's my mum!'

Holly couldn't bear it. She felt as if she were about to burst open. She pulled away from her dad and fled into the sitting room, letting the door slam shut behind her.

'Holly! Holly, darling!' He came after her and caught her in his arms again. She went limp.

'I'm sorry, pet, I know I shouldn't be slagging your mum off to you.' He sighed. 'Trouble is Sharon's never grown up.'

'Well, that's certainly true,' Sylvie said.

Holly rested her face against his shoulder. She was exhausted.

'Don't cry, love.' He stroked her hair. 'Everything's going to be all right, I promise you.' He held her close.

After a few moments, Holly lifted her head, sniffed and wiped her eyes with the back of her hand.

'OK?' he asked.

'Uh-huh.' She nodded. 'I mean, yes.'

'I suppose I'd better go and meet these folk. The Nightingales, is that how you call them?'

'They've been very good to me.'

'I'll need to thank them. And what do I owe them?'

'They wouldn't want you to pay anything, Dad. They're not like that.'

'I don't need to take charity from anybody. I've enough money of my own.'

Holly decided to let Colin and Nina fight it out with him, and led her dad into the kitchen. The family was sitting round the table drinking coffee. Nina and Colin got up at once.

'This is my dad,' said Holly awkwardly.

Nina and Colin shook hands and said they were very pleased to meet him. They also introduced Johnny, who reached his hand across the table. He was sitting with his plastered leg stuck out to the side.

'I've got to thank you,' began Holly's dad. He sounded awkward now and Holly felt sorry for him. He wasn't sure what to say. He cleared his throat. 'It was awful good of you to keep Holly all that time.'

'It's been a great pleasure,' said Nina.

'Indeed it has,' added Colin.

'Please do sit down,' invited Nina. 'Would you like some coffee or would you rather have tea?'

'Coffee's fine, thanks.'

He sat down with Holly beside him. He cleared his throat again.

'You must have spent money on Holly –'

'It was nothing.' Nina shook her head. 'Truly.'

'I'd like to pay you back.' Holly's dad was a proud man and he could be stubborn but then, as Holly knew, so could Nina.

'Mr Hamilton, she was our guest. We were happy to have her with us. She didn't cost us much and she was a great help.'

Holly wanted to kick her father under the table. She could see he was about say something else but she didn't want him going on about it any longer. Nina wouldn't like to take money from him.

'Well, if you're sure?' he said hesitantly.

'Totally!' Nina gave Holly a reassuring smile.

'So you came back early?' prompted Colin, moving the subject away from money.

Holly's dad nodded and then began to talk. It was as if a door had been opened – once he had started, Holly wondered if he'd ever stop. He'd returned to the flat, tried to phone them, couldn't get an answer and had gone to Glasgow immediately, where he'd talked to a number of people and found out all sorts of things that he hadn't known before. As he spoke he became angry, very angry.

'Holly's mum never let on to me that she was working at that place, the *Spike,* six nights a week till late. Three, four in the morning sometimes! And Holly all alone in that flat.'

'Mum couldn't help it,' put in Holly. Her dad patted her knee.

'I know, but she shouldn't have lied to me. She told me she had a job as a daytime waitress, was home at five for you every day.'

'She wouldn't have wanted to lose Holly,' said Nina quietly. 'I can understand that.'

'Maybe so. Doesn't excuse her, mind.'

'Of course not.'

Chrissie had also told Holly's dad about Lenny the Louse.

'He's got a record!'

Holly had never seen her dad so angry. For a moment she was worried that he might have a heart attack. His face had turned brick red.

'A police record?' asked Colin.

'Shoplifting. I'm not letting a man like that have anything to do with my daughter.'

'Mum likes him,' said Holly.

Her dad snorted. 'When they made her, the brains got left out.'

'That's not true!' cried Holly.

'Sorry, pet.' He took hold of her hand. 'But you must understand how *I* feel!'

'You do, don't you?' murmured Sylvie.

Nina said, 'You know, Holly's mum may not have known what Lenny was up to. Very likely not.'

'He wouldn't tell her,' agreed Holly. 'He's sleekit.'

'But she'd no business either, dumping you on any old person she came across at the station!' Holly's dad went on. Then he looked at Nina and his face flushed with embarrassment. 'I'm terribly sorry, Mrs –'

'Call me Nina. And my husband's Colin.'

'Joe.' Holly's dad muttered his own name. 'I wasn't meaning anything against you.'

'I realize that. I understand what a shock it must all have been to you.'

'You're telling me! It's when I think of Holly sitting there alone, late into the night –' He couldn't go on.

'Mum had to work,' muttered Holly.

'She could have looked for another job.'

'That might not be so easy,' countered Nina. 'Jobs can be scarce.'

'She's due back tomorrow, isn't she?' put in Colin.

'And I'll have plenty to say to her!' said Holly's dad.

'It might be wise to be wary of Lenny,' cautioned Colin.

'He doesn't carry a knife or anything,' cried Holly. 'And he's quite skinny.'

'Don't worry about him,' her dad returned grimly. And all of a sudden, his face broke into a smile at the thought of squaring up to a skinny Lenny. Colin and Nina laughed too.

'I want to see my mum.' Holly's voice wavered.

Her dad heaved a sigh. 'I know that.' He paused. 'But you can't go on living with her. You've got to accept that, love.'

'*Dad!*'

'No question! It's just not on.'

'But what am I going to do?'

'You're going to live with me.'

'How can I?'

'I've given up my job.'

'Honest?' What was her dad thinking of? Jobs didn't grow on trees – Nina just said!

'I'm not going back to the rig.'

Holly could hardly believe what she was hearing. 'But what about Mum?' Her mum depended on her.

'You can see her on Sundays. I've thought it all out and discussed it with the lady at the Social Services. The one who saw to you before, when they took you into care.'

'Rosemary?'

'Aye, that's her. I'll take you to Glasgow on Sundays to see your mum and if she wants she can come through here other afternoons during the week when you get out of school. I'm not stopping you seeing her. But you're *not* going to see Lenny.'

Holly didn't know what to feel. She'd never lived with her dad before and she didn't really like his flat very much. It was a kind of dreary place. Of course her dad had hardly ever lived there, only for a couple of weeks at a time, whereas her mum had put up coloured posters on their walls and bought fancy mugs and plates. She said they'd help to cheer the place up. Her mum's flat was a home – her dad's was just somewhere to stay.

As if her dad had read her mind he said, 'I'm going to sell the flat and get us a new place. Something nice.'

'But if you're not going back to the rig?' Holly was wondering what they would do for money.

'Give him a chance,' Sylvie muttered. 'He's got it all planned out.'

'My pal Ricky is giving me a job in his engineering firm.'

Holly thought about that for a moment. That meant

leaving Glasgow. Moving to Edinburgh. 'I'd have to go a new school.'

'I'm sure you'd settle in quickly, Holly,' said Nina. 'And you could come and visit us whenever you wanted to.'

Holly looked at Nina. 'I could, couldn't I?'

'Of course!'

Holly smiled. 'And maybe you could come and give a talk at my new school?'

'Maybe I could,' said Nina, returning the smile.

Twenty-One

Nina took Holly into her study before she left. She said she had some books to give her, which she did. But she also wanted to talk to her.

'Sit down a minute, love.'

They sat facing each other.

'I just want you to know that I meant it when I said you could come here any time, Holly. Or ring me up. If you need help with anything. Anything at all. You'd do that, wouldn't you?'

Holly nodded.

'Some things in your new life are going to be a bit difficult –'

'My mum,' interrupted Holly.

'I know. But I think you realize your dad couldn't let things carry on as they were?'

'My mum's not bad!'

'Of course she's not. You'll still see her. You'll probably have a lovely time with her on Sundays.'

'She can be fun. She says we're more like sisters.'

'Perhaps that's the problem…' said Sylvie.

'And, as your dad said, she can come through to Edinburgh to see you.'

'It's just that she doesn't quite get things sometimes. It's hard to explain.'

Nina nodded. She understood.

'You know I've loved having you to stay with us?'

'I've really liked being with you.'

They hugged each other and Holly blinked back a tear. She'd cried more in the past two weeks than she'd ever cried in her life! She hated saying all these goodbyes.

'It's not for ever,' Sylvie reminded her.

'Thanks, Nina. For all the things…' Holly's voice trailed away. She couldn't quite find the words for what she wanted to say.

'That's all right. We'll miss you, Johnny too! Yes, he will, though he'd never say so. Colin and I have often thought it would have been good for him to have had a sister – but that didn't happen. We'll see you soon though, love.'

Holly went into the kitchen to say goodbye to Johnny. She was certainly not going to hug him.

'I should hope not!' said Sylvie.

'So you're off?' he said.

'Uh-huh.'

'Who am I going to play chess with?' Johnny was fiddling with a pencil. He'd been in the middle of a Sudoku.

'What about your dad?'

'He's always too busy.'

'Tim then?'

'He doesn't play.'

'Mike?'

'He's rubbish.'

'And your mum hates it.'

Johnny tapped the pencil on the table. Then he asked in an off-hand way, 'When do you think you'll be coming back?'

'Soon, probably.'

'OK, see you!'

'See you!' she said and went out to join her dad, smiling.

Nina and Colin stood on the doorstep to wave goodbye. Holly twisted right round in her seat to wave back. She gulped to get rid of the lump in her throat. They rounded the corner of the street and then the house and the Nightingales were left behind.

Just after they'd turned a big square car passed them going in the opposite direction. A woman who Holly thought must be Evangeline was at the wheel, and in the passenger seat sat Mariposa as large as life. Holly started to laugh.

'What's the joke, pet?' asked her father.

'It's just this American woman,' she started and then stopped. Her dad wouldn't understand the joke. It didn't matter. They had special jokes of their own that they laughed about.

A few minutes later they were pulling up outside her dad's flat. He carried her bags and they climbed the stairs together.

'Here we are then, Holly!' he said, as he unlocked the door.

The flat wasn't as cold and dreary as Holly had remembered. Her dad had put on the heating so that it felt quite warm and cosy. And he'd bought a bunch of flame-coloured tulips that he'd stuck into a jar.

'We'll need to buy a couple of vases,' he said.

'The tulips are pretty.' She touched one of the flowers. She loved their bright colour.

'We'll go out and do a big shop and get ourselves some nice things. Would you like that?'

She nodded.

'I know it's not posh like the Nightingales' house but it'll do us till we get something else.'

'Their place isn't very posh. Just big.'

'We'll start looking next week. We might get a flat looking over the sea.'

'I'd like that.'

'And we'll go out somewhere nice tonight and have ourselves a slap-up meal. What would you fancy? Italian? Indian? Chinese? You choose!'

'Maybe Italian?'

'Italian it is then. Why don't you go and unpack your things, pet?'

Holly took her bags through to the bedroom and sat down on the bed. Everything had happened so terribly fast in the end that she hadn't had time to think properly. Her head had been birling like a top. Now it had calmed down and she felt quiet.

She thought about the Nightingales. She'd been sorry to leave them even though she'd wanted to come with her dad.

'You can go and see Nina any time,' Sylvie reminded her. 'She said so. They're not that far away. And you'll see your mum on Sunday.'

'If she comes back. She and Lenny the Louse might have relocated to Bulgaria.'

'Don't talk daft! She'll come back. She always does, you know that.'

'She won't like it, me being with my dad.'

'Maybe not. But I think she'll understand. With her working at the *Spike*, well, it's difficult for her, isn't it?'

The door bell rang. Holly lifted her head to listen. She heard the flat door opening and then the sound of Mrs McGinty's voice.

'I thought somebody was moving about in here. So you're back.'

'Aye, I'm back.'

'And what about that lassie of yours?'

'She's here too.'

'Is she staying with you?'

'She is.'

'If I were you I wouldn't let her go back to that besom of a mother!'

'I must go, Mrs McGinty.'

'I was just wanting to make sure there hadn't been a break-in.'

'There hasn't. Thanks.'

The door closed.

Holly's dad came into her room.

'The sooner we get away from that woman the better!' he said.

Holly grinned. The world was full of busybodies – Mrs McGinty, Mrs Blackie, Evangeline, Mariposa…

Her dad came and sat down on the bed beside her.

'It's going to be all right, you know, Holly,' he began. 'You and me. It'll just take us a wee bit of time getting used to living together. You'll still see your mum, I won't go back on my promise. But you know I couldn't let you stay with her.' There was a pause. This seemed hard for him. 'You do, don't you?'

'I suppose.'

'I couldn't.' He sounded upset.

'No, I do know, Dad.'

'Good. And if you want to see your new friends you can.' Her dad took a deep breath so she knew he must be getting ready to say something important. 'I love you, Holly.'

'Love you too, Dad.'

He smiled at her, and she smiled right back. 'That's great, pet. We're going to be pals, aren't we?'

Holly nodded.

Then she turned and gave her father a hug.

She knew Sylvie would approve of that.